Puffin Books
Editor: Kaye

THE FIRST FOUR YEARS

Most of us who have read and loved all seven of the
books about Laura's pioneer childhood in America,
beginning with *Little House In the Big Woods*, when she
was only a little girl, will have thought sadly,
as they finished *These Happy Golden Years*, by which
time she had grown up into a spirited and pretty young
lady: 'And that's the very end.'

But luckily for us there is just a little more,
a story which Laura wrote down in three orange notebooks
when she was a very old lady, the story of the early
years of her marriage to Almanzo Wilder. And this
you have here in *The First Four Years*.

It tells how Laura and Almanzo (who was now
known as Manly) were married quietly and went
straight to their new home so that Manly could be
getting on with the harvest the very next day. Laura was
delighted with their bright and shining little house,
and she loved setting it to rights in the mornings
and making it spick and span and homely – but we still
see flashes of the old Laura in the very young wife
who forgot to put sugar in the pie the day the
threshers were coming to lunch, and who enjoyed
playing in the snow with her sledge.

Laura was busy all day long now with cooking,
baking, churning, sweeping, washing, ironing and
mending, and there was deep happiness when their
little daughter Rose arrived to complete the family, but
there were also hardships and problems over money,
as well as failed crops and disappointments, before
Laura, Manly and little Rose found their way to the
prosperous and happy farm where they lived until
the end of their days.

LAURA INGALLS WILDER

The First Four Years

with an Epilogue by Rose Wilder Lane
from *On the Way Home*

PUFFIN BOOKS

Puffin Books, Penguin Books Ltd,
Harmondsworth, Middlesex, England
Penguin Books, 625 Madison Avenue,
New York, New York 10022, U.S.A.
Penguin Books Australia Ltd,
Ringwood, Victoria, Australia
Penguin Books Canada Ltd,
2801 John Street, Markham,
Ontario, Canada L3R 1B4
Penguin Books (N.Z.) Ltd,
182–190 Wairau Road,
Auckland 10, New Zealand

The First Four Years first published in the U.S.A. by
Harper & Row 1971
Text copyright © Roger Lea MacBride, 1971
On the Way Home first published in the U.S.A. by
Harper & Row 1962
Copyright © Roger Lea MacBride, 1962
Linking passages on pages 85 and 97,
and map on page 96, first published by
Lutterworth Press 1973
Published in Puffin Books 1978
Reprinted 1979
Copyright © Lutterworth Press, 1973
All rights reserved

Made and printed in Great Britain by
C. Nicholls & Company Ltd
Set in Monotype Plantin

Contents

Introduction

This tale begins where *These Happy Golden Years* ends. It tells of the struggle of Laura and Almanzo Wilder during their first years of marriage and is the next chapter in the story begun in Laura's childhood eight books earlier. Its events occur before those described in *On the Way Home* – Laura's diary account of the little family's adventures when they moved by wagon from Dakota Territory to Missouri in 1894.

The manuscript of *The First Four Years* was discovered among Laura's papers. She had pencilled it in three orange-covered school tablets bought long ago from the Springfield Grocer Company for a nickel each. Laura wrote the first drafts of her previous books in the same way. My own guess is that she wrote this one in the late 1940s and that after Almanzo died, she lost interest in revising and completing it for publication. Because she didn't do so, there is a difference from the earlier books in the way the story is told.

An important part tells of the birth and childhood of Rose, Laura and Almanzo's daughter. Rose was my dearest friend and mentor. I met Rose when I was a young boy and later became her lawyer. My wife and I were close to her for many years. She gave me the manuscript of this book for safekeeping, and after her death in 1968, I brought it to Harper & Row. After considerable thought about the countless children and adults who have read the 'Little House' books, and concern for what Rose and Laura might have wanted, the editors at Harper and I all agreed that Laura's original draft should be published as she had first written it in her orange notebooks.

Rose grew up to be a famous author who carried on Laura's pioneer spirit by having many adventures in America and abroad. She wrote a number of fascinating books about this country and about faraway places like Albania, and she became well known the world over. But Rose grew up in a time when ladies did not consciously seek fame. She chose to shed light on the lives of others instead of her own, and so this book about her mother, father and herself had to wait until after her death to be published.

Rose (who became Mrs Rose Wilder Lane) led a full and busy life. After her mother died, she wrote the setting for *On the Way Home*. She also wrote a number of magazine articles, some of which were published as the *Woman's Day Book of American Needlework*. She worked at length on a major book yet to be published, and she was sent to Vietnam as a war correspondent in 1965 when she was seventy-eight years old! Rose read constantly and knew more about any subject I can think of than any person I ever knew. A week before she was to set off on a world tour at age eighty-one, her heart stopped suddenly, at her home of thirty years in Danbury, Connecticut. The night before, she had sat up in jovial and lively conversation with friends after making them a baking of her famous bread.

But what happened after the events described in both *The First Four Years* and *On the Way Home* – after Laura, Almanzo and Rose reached 'The Land of the Big Red Apple'?

There in the Ozarks, Almanzo built by hand, with care and precision, a charming country house on land that Laura later named Rocky Ridge Farm. They lived and successfully farmed right there for long and happy lifetimes, Almanzo's ending in 1949 at age ninety-two, and Laura's in 1957 at age ninety. Their home was made sturdily to last for always, and the lucky people who go to Mansfield, Missouri, may see that happy home with its fossils in its chimney rock, much furniture hand-made by Almanzo, and many other treasures. Pa's violin, Mary's organ and Laura's lovely sewing box are there as well as some of Rose's possessions. Rocky Ridge Farm is now a permanent nonprofit exhibit. If you go, the curators, who loved and knew the Wilders personally, will take you around and tell you details that may not be in the 'Little House' books, to help you better to know Laura, Almanzo and Rose.

We all wish there were more of Laura's stories. We have come to know and cherish their qualities of character and spirit. They have entered our lives and given them meaning. But if there cannot be more, may we make life stories of our own worthy of hers.

ROGER LEA MACBRIDE
Charlottesville, Virginia
July 1970

Prologue

The stars hung luminous and low over the prairie. Their light showed plainly the crests of the rises in the gently rolling land, but left the lower draws and hollows in deeper shadows.

A light buggy drawn by a team of quick-stepping dark horses passed swiftly over the road which was only a dim trace across the grasslands. The buggy top was down, and the stars shone softly on the dark blur of the driver and the white-clothed form in the seat beside him, and were reflected in the waters of Silver Lake that lay within its low, grass-grown banks.

The night was sweet with strong, dewy fragrance of the wild prairie roses that grew in masses beside the way.

A sweet contralto voice rose softly on the air above the lighter patter of the horses' feet, as horses and buggy and dim figures passed along the way. And it seemed as if the stars and water and roses were listening to the voice, so quiet were they, for it was of them it sang.

> In the starlight, in the starlight,
> At the daylight's dewy close,
> When the nightingale is singing
> His last love song to the rose;
> In the calm clear night of summer
> When the breezes gently play,
> From the glitter of our dwelling
> We will softly steal away.

> Where the silv'ry waters murmur
> By the margin of the sea,
> In the starlight, in the starlight,
> We will wander gay and free.

For it was June, the roses were in bloom over the prairie lands, and lovers were abroad in the still, sweet evenings which were so quiet after the winds had hushed at sunset.

1. The First Year

It was a hot afternoon with a strong wind from the south, but out on the Dakota prairie in 1885 no one minded the hot sunshine or the hard winds. They were to be expected: a natural part of life. And so the swiftly trotting horses drawing the shining black-top buggy swung around the corner of Pierson's livery barn, making the turn from the end of Main Street to the country road Monday afternoon at four o'clock.

Looking from a window of the low, three-room claim shanty a half mile away, Laura saw them coming. She was basting cambric lining to the bodice pieces of her new black cashmere dress and had just time to put on her hat and pick up her gloves when the brown horses and the buggy stopped at the door.

It was a pretty picture Laura made standing at the door of the rough claim shanty, the brown August grass under her feet and the young cottonwoods standing in their square around the yard.

Her dress of pink lawn with its small sprigs of blue flowers just cleared her toes. The skirt was full, and tucked to the waist. The little tight waist with long sleeves and high neck had a bit of lace at the throat. The sage-green, rough-straw poke bonnet lined with blue silk softly framed her pink cheeks and her large blue eyes with the bangs of her brown hair above them.

Manly said nothing of all this, but he helped her into the buggy and tucked the linen lap robe carefully about her to keep off the dust. Then he tightened the reins and they dashed away for an unexpected week-day afternoon drive. South twelve miles across bare prairie to lakes Henry and Thompson, along the narrow neck of land between them where chokecherries and wild grapes grew. Then over the prairie again east and north to Spirit Lake fifteen miles away. Forty or fifty miles in all, but always 'around the square' to come home.

The buggy top was up to make a shade from the heat of the sun; the horses' manes and tails flew out on the wind; jack rabbits ran and prairie chickens scuttled out of sight in the grass. Striped gophers ducked into their holes and wild ducks flew overhead from one lake to another. Breaking a somewhat lengthy silence, Manly said, 'Can't we be married soon? If you don't want a big wedding, and you would be willing, we could be married right away. When I was back in Minnesota last winter, my sister started planning a big church wedding for us. I told her we didn't want it, and to give up the idea, but she hasn't changed her mind. She is coming out here with my mother, to take charge of our wedding. But harvest is right on hand. It will be an awfully busy time and I'd like us to be settled first.'

Laura twisted the bright gold ring with its pearl-and-garnet setting around and around on the forefinger of her left hand. It was a pretty ring and she liked having it, but ... 'I've been thinking,' she said. 'I don't want to marry a farmer. I have always said I never would. I do wish you would do something else. There are chances in town now while it is so new and growing.'

Again there was a little silence; then Manly asked, 'Why don't you want to marry a farmer?' And Laura replied, 'Because a farm is such a hard place for a woman. There are so many chores for her to do, and harvest help and threshers to cook for. Besides a farmer never has any money. He can never make any because the people in towns tell him what they will pay for what he has to sell and then they charge him what they please for what he has to buy. It is not fair.'

Manly laughed. 'Well, as the Irishman said, "Everything is evened up in this world. The rich have their ice in the summer but the poor get theirs in the winter."'

Laura refused to make a joke of it. She said, 'I don't always want to be poor and work hard while the people in town take it easy and make money off us.'

'But you've got it all wrong,' Manly told her seriously. 'Farmers are the only ones who are independent. How long would a merchant last if farmers didn't trade with him? There is a strife between them to please the farmer. They have to take trade away from each other in order to make more money, while all a farmer has to do is to sow another field if he wants to make a little extra.

'I have fifty acres of wheat this year. It is enough for me, but if you will come live on the farm, I will break the ground this fall and sow another fifty acres next spring.

'I can raise more oats too and so raise more horses, and it pays to raise horses.

'You see, on a farm it all depends on what a man is willing to do. If he is willing to work and give his attention to his farm, he can make more money than the men in town and all the time be his own boss.'

Again there was a silence, a rather sceptical silence on Laura's part, broken at last by Manly, who said, 'If you'll try it for three years and I haven't made a success in farming by that time, I'll quit and do anything you want me to do. I promise that at the end of three years we will quit farming if I have not made such a success that you are willing to keep on.'

And Laura consented to try it for three years. She liked the horses and enjoyed the freedom and spaciousness of the wide prairie land, with the wind forever waving the tall wild grass in the sloughs and rustling through the short curly buffalo grass, so green on the upland swells in spring and so silvery grey and brown in summer. It was all so sweet and fresh. In early spring the wild violets carpeted and made fragrant the little hollows of the grassland, and in June the wild prairie roses blossomed everywhere. Two quarter sections of this land, each with 160 acres of rich black soil, would be theirs, for Manly had already proven up on a homestead and he also had a tree claim on which he was growing the ten acres of trees required by law to get title. The 3405 trees were planted about eight feet apart each way. Between the two claims lay a school section where anyone could cut the hay, first come first served.

It would be much more fun living on the land than on the town street with neighbours so close on each side, and if only Manly were right – Well, she had promised to try the farm anyway.

'The house on the tree claim will be finished in a couple of weeks,' Manly was saying. 'Let's be married the next week. It will be the last week in August and before the rush of harvest begins. Let's just drive over to Reverend Brown's and then go home to our new house.'

But Laura objected to this because she would not be paid for the last month of her school teaching until October and needed the money for clothes.

'What's the matter with the clothes you have?' Manly asked. 'You always look nice and if we are married suddenly, that way we won't need fine clothes.

'If we give Mother time enough, she and the girls will come out from the east and we will have to have a big wedding in the church. I can't afford the expense and your one month's salary would not be enough for you.'

This was a surprise, for Laura had not thought of such a thing. In the wild new country, the folks back east never seemed to be real and certainly were not considered in the making of plans, but she remembered with something of a shock that

Manly's folks back in eastern Minnesota were well off and that one sister had a homestead claim near by. They would be sure to come if they knew the wedding date, and his mother had asked for that in her latest letter.

She could not ask her Pa to go to any expense for the wedding. It was all he could do to keep up with the family expenses until there would be some return from their 160 acres of wild land. Nothing much could be expected from the raw sod the first year it was turned over, and his farmland was newly broke.

There seemed no other way than to be married suddenly because of the help it would be to have a home and housekeeper in the rush of fall work coming on. Manly's mother would understand and not be offended. It would be thought the right and sensible way to do by the neighbours and friends, for they were all engaged in the same struggle to establish themselves in their homes on the new prairie land.

And so on Thursday, the twenty-fifth of August, at ten o'clock in the morning, the quick-stepping brown horses and the buggy with the shining top flashed around the corner at Pierson's livery barn, came swiftly over the half mile, and drew up at the door of the little claim house in its hollow square of young cottonwoods.

Laura stood at the door, her Ma and Pa on either hand, her two sisters grouped behind her.

They all gaily tried to help her into the buggy. Her wedding dress was the new black cashmere she had thought would be so serviceable, for a married woman should have a black dress.

All her other clothing and her few girlhood treasures had been packed in a trunk and were waiting in Manly's newly finished house.

As Laura looked back, Ma, Pa, and Carrie and Grace were grouped among the young trees. They threw kisses and waved their hands. Bright green leaves of the cottonwoods waved too in the stronger wind of afternoon and there was a little choke in Laura's throat for they seemed to be saying good-bye, and she saw her Ma brush her hand quickly across her eyes.

Manly understood, for he covered Laura's hand with one of his and pressed it strongly.

The preacher lived on his homestead two miles away and it seemed to Laura the longest drive she had ever taken, and yet it was over all too soon. Once in the front room, the ceremony was quickly performed. Mr Brown came hurriedly in, slipping on his coat. His wife and his daughter, Ida, Laura's dearest friend, with her betrothed, were the witnesses and those present.

Laura and Manly were married for better or worse, for richer or poorer.

Then back to the old home for a noon dinner, and in the midst of good wishes and cheerful good-byes, once more into the buggy and away for the new home on the other side of town. The first year was begun.

The summer wind blew softly, and the sunshine was bright where it shone through the east windows that first morning. It was an early sun, but breakfast was even earlier, for Manly must not be late at the Webbs' for the threshing. All the neighbours would be there. Since they would expect Mr Webb to give them a good day's work in exchange, as their turns with the threshers came, no one could afford to be late and hold up the gang at Webb's place. So the first breakfast in the new home was a hurried affair. Then Manly drove away with the brown horses hitched to the lumber wagon, and Laura was alone for the day.

It would be a busy day, there was so much to do putting the little new house in order.

Before beginning, Laura looked the place over with all the pride of possession.

There was the kitchen-dining-living room, all in one but so

nicely proportioned and so cannily furnished that it answered all purposes delightfully.

The front door in the north-east corner of the room opened onto the horseshoe-shaped drive before the house. Just south of it was the east window where the morning sun shone in. In the centre of the south wall was another bright window.

The drop-leaf table stood against the west wall with one leaf raised and a chair at either end. It was covered with Ma's bright red-and-white checked tablecloth on which stood the remains of the early breakfast. A door at the end of the table led into the storm shed, and there was Almanzo's cook-stove with pots and frying pans on the walls. Then there was a window and a back door that opened towards the south.

Just across the corner from the door into the shed was the pantry door. And such a pantry! Laura was so delighted for several minutes, admiring it. It was narrow, of course, but long. Opposite her at the far end was a full-sized window, and just outside the window stood a young cottonwood tree, its small green leaves fluttering in the morning wind.

Inside before the window was a broad work shelf just the right height at which to stand. On the wall at the right a strip of board ran the whole length and in it were driven nails on which to hang dishpans, dish towels, colanders, and other kitchen utensils.

But the wall to the left was all a beautiful cabinet.

Manly had found a carpenter of the old days who though old and slow did beautiful work, and the pantry had been his pride and a labour of love to Manly.

The wall was shelved the whole length. The top shelf was only a short space from the ceiling, and from it down, spaces between the shelves were wider until there was room for tall pitchers and other dishes to stand on the lower shelf. Beneath the lowest shelf was a row of drawers as well made and fitted as boughten furniture. There was a large wide drawer to hold a baking of bread. There was one drawer that already held a whole sack of white flour, a smaller one with graham flour, another with corn meal, a large shallow one for packages, and two others: one already filled with white sugar and the other one with brown. And one for Manly's wedding present of silver knives and forks and spoons. Laura was so proud of them. Underneath the drawers was an open space to the floor and here stood the stone cookie-jar, the doughnut jar, and the jar of lard. Here also stood the tall stone churn and the dasher. The churn looked rather large when the only cow giving milk was the small fawn-coloured heifer Pa had given them for a wedding present, but there would be more cream later when Manly's cow should be fresh.

In the centre of the pantry floor, a trap door opened into the cellar.

The door into the bedroom was just across the corner from the front door. On the wall at the foot of the bed was a high shelf for hats. A curtain hung from the edge of the shelf to the floor, and on the wall behind it were hooks for hanging clothes. And there was a carpet on the floor!

The pine floor of the front room and pantry were painted a bright clean yellow. The walls of all the house were white plaster, and the pine woodwork was satin-smooth and oiled and varnished in its natural colour.

It was a bright and shining little house and it was really all theirs, Laura thought. It belonged to just Manly and her.

The house had been built on the tree claim, looking forward to the time when the small switches of trees should be grown. Already Manly and Laura seemed to see it sitting in a beautiful grove of cottonwoods and elms and maples which were already planted along beside the road. The hopeful little trees stood in the half-circle of the drive before the house. They were hovering close to each side and at the back. Oh, surely, if they were tended well, it would not be long before they sheltered and protected the little house from the summer's heat and the winter's cold and the winds that were always blowing! But Laura could not stand idly in the pantry dreaming and watching the cottonwood leaves blowing. There was work to be done. She cleared the breakfast table quickly. It was only a step from it to the pantry where everything was arranged on the shelves as it belonged; the dirty dishes she piled in the dishpan on the work shelf before the window. The tea kettle of hot water on the stove was handy too, and soon everything was clean and the door closed upon the pantry in perfect order.

Next Laura polished the stove with a flannel cloth, swept the floor, dropped the table leaf and spread a clean, bright red tablecloth over it. The cloth had a beautiful border and made the table an ornament fit for anyone's front room.

In the corner between the window to the east and the window to the south was a small stand-table with an easy armchair at one side and a small rocker at the other. Above it suspended from the ceiling was a glass lamp with glittering pendants. That was the parlour part of the room, and when the copies of Scott's and Tennyson's poems were on the stand it would be complete. She would have some geraniums growing in cans on the windows soon and then it would be simply beautiful.

But the windows must be washed. They were splattered with plaster and paint from the house-building. And how Laura did hate to wash windows!

Just then there was a rap at the screen door, and Hattie, the hired girl from the farm adjoining, was there. Manly had stopped as he drove to the threshing and asked that she come and wash the windows when she could be spared!

So Hattie washed the windows while Laura tidied the little bedroom and unpacked her trunk. Her hat was already on the shelf and the wedding dress hanging on its hook behind the curtain.

There were only a few dresses to hang up, the fawn-coloured silk with the black stripes, and the brown poplin she had made. They had been worn many times but were still nice. There was the pink lawn with the blue flowers. It would not be warm enough to wear that more than once or twice again this summer. Then there was the grey calico work dress to change with the blue she was wearing.

And her last-winter's coat looked very good hanging on the hook beside Manly's overcoat. It would do for the winter that was coming. She didn't want to be an expense to Manly right at the beginning. She wanted to help him prove that farming was as good as any other business. This was such a lovely little home, so much better than living on a town street.

Oh, she did hope Manly was right, and she smiled as she repeated to herself, 'Everything is evened up in this world.'

Manly was late home, for threshers worked as long as there was daylight to see by. Supper was on the table when he came in from doing the chores, and as they ate, he told Laura the threshers would come next day, would be there at noon for dinner.

It would be the first dinner in the new home and she must cook it for the threshers! To encourage her, Manly said, 'You'll get along all right. And you can never learn younger.'

Now Laura had always been a pioneer girl rather than a farmer's daughter, always moving on to new places before the fields grew large, so a gang of men as large as a threshing crew to feed by herself was rather dismaying. But if she was going to be a farmer's wife that was all in the day's work.

So early next morning she began to plan and prepare for dinner. She had brought a baking of bread from home, and with some hot corn bread there would be plenty. Pork and potatoes were on hand and she had put some navy beans to soak the night before. There was a pieplant in the garden; she must make a couple of pies. The morning flew too quickly, but when the men came in at noon from the thresher, dinner was on the table.

The table was in the centre of the room with both leaves raised to make room, but even then some of the men must wait for the second table. They were all very hungry but there was plenty of food, though something seemed to be wrong with the beans. Lacking her Ma's watchful eye, Laura had not cooked them enough and they were hard. And when it came to the pie – Mr Perry, a neighbour of Laura's parents, tasted his first. Then he lifted the top crust, and reaching for the sugar bowl, spread sugar thickly over his piece of pie. 'That is the way I like it,' he said. 'If there is no sugar in the pie, then every fellow can sweeten his own as much as he likes without hurting the cook's feelings.'

Mr Perry had made the meal a jolly one. He told tales of when he was a boy in Pennsylvania. His mother, he said, used to take five beans and a kettle of water to make bean soup. The kettle was so large that after they had eaten all the bean broth and bread they could, they had to take off their coats and dive for a bean if they wanted one. Everyone laughed and talked and was very friendly, but Laura felt mortified about her beans and her pie without any sugar in. She had been so hurried when she made the pies; but how could she have been so careless? Pieplant was so sour, that first taste must have been simply terrible.

The wheat had turned out only ten bushels to the acre, and wheat was selling at fifty cents a bushel. Not much of a crop. It had been too dry and the price was low. But the field of oats had yielded enough to furnish grain for the horses with some to spare. There was hay in great stacks, plenty for the horses and cows and some to sell.

Manly was very cheerful and already planning for next year. He was in a great hurry to begin the fall ploughing and the breaking of new sod land, for he was determined to double his acreage next year – or more, if possible. The wheat for seed was stored in the claim shanty on the homestead, for there was no grinery on the tree claim. The rest of the wheat was sold.

Now was a busy, happy time. Manly was early in the field, ploughing, and Laura was busy all day with cooking, baking, churning, sweeping, washing, ironing and mending. The washing and ironing were hard for her to do. She was small and slender but her little hands and wrists were strong and she got it done. Afternoons, she always put on a clean dress and sat in the parlour corner of the front room sewing, or knitting on Manly's socks.

Sundays they always went for a buggy ride and as the horses trotted along the prairie roads Laura and Manly would sing the old singing-school songs. Their favourite was 'Don't Leave the Farm, Boys'.

> You talk of the mines of Australia,
> They've wealth in red gold, without doubt;
> But, ah! there is gold on the farm, boys –
> If only you'll shovel it out.

Chorus:

> Don't be in a hurry to go!
> Don't be in a hurry to go!
> Better risk the old farm awhile longer,
> Don't be in a hurry to go!

And Laura thought of the golden wheat stored in the homestead claim shanty and she was glad.

The drives were short these days for the ploughing was hard work for pretty, quick-stepping Skip and Barnum, the driving team.

Manly said they were not large enough to do all the breaking of the new sod land. One day he came home from town leading two large horses hitched behind the wagon, and they were drawing a new sulky breaking plough. Now Manly said he could hitch all four horses to the big plough. Then there would be no trouble in getting the land broke for his crops next year. The horses had been a bargain because their owner was in a hurry to sell and get away. He had sold the relinquishment of his homestead to a man from the east and was going farther west and take up another claim where government land could still be found.

The sulky plough had cost fifty-five dollars, but Manly had only paid half down and given a note for the rest to be paid next year. The plough turned a furrow sixteen inches wide in the tough grass sod and would pay for itself in the extra acres Manly could get ready for crops since he could ride instead of walking and holding a narrow walking plough.

After that Laura would go out in the morning and help hitch the four horses to the plough. She learned to drive them and handle the plough too and sometimes would plough several times around the field. She thought it great fun.

Shortly after this Manly came from town again and behind the wagon was a small iron-grey pony. 'Here,' he said to Laura, 'is something for you to play with. And don't let me hear any more about your father not letting you learn to ride horses. This one is gentle and won't hurt you.'

Laura looked at the pony and loved it. 'I'll call her Trixy,' she said. The pony's feet were small and her legs fine and flat. Her head was small with a fine mealy nose and ears pointed and alert. Her eyes were large and quick and gentle, and her mane and tail were long and thick. That night after supper, Laura chose her saddle from the descriptions and pictures in Montgomery Ward's catalogue and made the order for it ready to mail the first trip to town. She could hardly wait for the saddle to come but she shortened the two weeks' time by making friends with Trixy. It was a beautiful all-leather saddle, tan-coloured and fancy-stitched with nickel trimmings.

'And now,' said Manly, 'I'll put the saddle on Trixy and you and she can learn together. I'm sure she'll be gentle even if she never has been ridden, but better head her onto the ploughed ground. It will be harder going for her – so she won't be so frisky – and a soft place for you to light if you fall off.' So when Laura was safely in the saddle, her left foot in the leather slipper stirrup, her right knee over the saddle horn with the leaf-horn fitting snugly about it, Manly let go the bridle and Laura and Trixy went out on the ploughed ground. Trixy was good and did her best to please even though she was afraid of Laura's skirt blowing in the wind. Laura didn't fall off, and day after day they learned horseback riding together.

It was growing late in the fall. The nights were frosty and soon the ground would freeze. The breaking of the new fifty-acre field was nearly finished. There were no Sunday afternoon drives now. Skip and Barnum were working too hard at the ploughing to be driven. They must have their day of rest. Instead, there were long horseback rides, for Manly had a saddle pony of his own, and Fly and Trixy, having nothing else to do, were always ready to go. Laura and Trixy had learned to foxtrot and to lope together. The little short lope would land them from the side of the road across the wheel track onto the grass-covered middle. Another jump would cross the other wheel track. Trixy would light so springily on her dainty feet that there was never a jar.

One day as they were loping down a road Manly said, 'Oh, yes! Trixy can jump short and quick, but Fly can run away from her' – and Fly started. Laura bent low over Trixy's neck, touched her with her whip, and imitated, as near as she could manage, a cowboy yell. Trixy shot ahead like a streak, leaving Fly behind. Laura stopped her and sat a little breathless until Manly came up. But when Manly protested at the sudden start she said airily, 'Oh, Trixy told me she was going in plenty of time.'

After that it was proven many times that Trixy was faster – often on a twenty-mile ride over the open prairie before breakfast.

It was a carefree, happy time, for two people thoroughly in sympathy can do pretty much as they like.

To be sure, now and then Laura thought about the short crop and wondered. Once she even saved the cream carefully and sent a jar of fresh butter to town for sale, thinking it would help pay for the groceries Manly was getting. With the butter, she sent five dozen eggs, for the little flock of hens, picking their living around the barn and the straw stacks and in the fields, were laying wonderfully well.

But Manly brought the butter back. Not a store in town wanted it at any price and he had been able to get only five cents a dozen for the eggs. Laura couldn't help any in that way. But why worry? Manly didn't.

When the breaking was finished, the hay barn back of the house was made more snug for winter. It was a warm place for the stock, with hay stacked tightly on each side against the skeleton frame. Hay was stacked even over the roof, about four feet thick at the eaves and a little thicker at the peak of the roof to give plenty of slant to shed water.

With a long hay knife, Manly had cut two holes through the haystack on the south side of the barn. Then he had put windows over the holes inside the barn, for he said, the stock must have light even with the door shut.

When the barn was made snug, it was butchering time.

But Ole Larsen, the neighbour across the road, butchered first. Mr Larsen was always borrowing. It was the cause of disagreement between Manly and Laura, for Laura objected to tools and machinery being used and broken and not returned. When she saw Manly going afoot to the back end of Ole

Larsen's field to get some machine that should have been at his own barn, she was angry, but Manly said one must be neighbourly.

So when Mr Larsen came over to borrow the large barrel in which to scald his hog in the butchering, she told him to take it. Manly was in town but she knew he would lend it.

In a few minutes Mr Larsen came back to borrow her wash boiler to heat water to scald the hog. Soon he was back again to borrow her butcher knives for the work, and again a little later to get her knife whetstone to sharpen the knives. Grimly Laura said to herself if he came next to borrow their fat hog to kill she would let him have it. But he had a hog of his own.

And after all that, he did not bring over a bit of fresh meat as good neighbours always did.

A few days later Manly butchered his fat hog and Laura had her first experience making sausage, head cheese, and lard all by herself. Hams and shoulders and spareribs were frozen in the storm shed and fat meat was salted down in a small barrel.

Laura found doing work alone very different from helping Ma. But it was part of her job and she must do it, though she did hate the smell of hot lard, and the sight of so much fresh meat ruined her appetite for any of it.

It was at this time that the directors of the school were able to pay Laura the salary for the last month she had taught. The money made Laura feel quite rich and she began planning how she should spend it. Manly told her if she bought a colt with it she could double the money in a short time by selling it when it was grown. So that was what they decided to do, and Manly bought a bay two-year-old that promised to grow out well.

Laura didn't bother to name the colt. It was just to be sold again, so what was the use? But the animal was fed well, brushed and cared for, to make it grow well.

One blustery day Manly started early for town, leaving Laura very much alone. She was used to being the only person on the place and thought nothing of it, but the wind was so cold and raw that she had not opened the front door. It was still locked from the night. In the middle of the morning, busy with her work, Laura looked out the window and saw a little bunch of horsemen coming across the prairie from the southeast. She wondered why they were not travelling on the road. As they came nearer she saw there were five of them, and they were Indians.

Laura had seen Indians often, without fear, but she felt a quick jump of her heart as they came up to the house and without knocking tried to open the front door. She was glad the door was locked, and she slipped quickly into the back room and locked the outside door there.

The Indians came around the house to the back door and tried to open that. Then seeing Laura through the window they made signs for her to open the door indicating that they would not hurt her. But Laura shook her head and told them to go away. Likely they only wanted something to eat, but still one could never tell. It was only three years ago that the Indians nearly went on the warpath a little way west, and even now they often threatened the railroad camps.

She wouldn't open the door but watched them as they jabbered together. She couldn't catch a word that she could understand, and she was afraid. They weren't acting right. Why didn't they go away!

Instead they were going to the barn – and her new saddle was hanging in the barn and Trixy was there ... Trixy! Her pet and comrade!

Laura was afraid; in the house there was comparative safety, for they'd hardly break in. But now Laura was angry too, and as always she acted quickly. Flinging the door open, she ran to the barn, and standing in the door, ordered the Indians out.

One of them was feeling the leather of her beautiful saddle and one was in the stall with Trixy. Trixy was afraid too. She never liked strangers and she was pulling at her halter and trembling.

The other Indians were examining Manly's saddle and the buggy harness with its bright nickel trimmings, but they all came and gathered around Laura just outside the door. She stormed at them and stamped her foot. Her head was bare and her long brown braids of hair blew out on the wind while her purple eyes flashed fire as always when she was angry or very much excited.

The Indians only stared for a moment; then one of them grunted an unintelligible word and laid his hand on Laura's arm. Quick as a flash she slapped his face with all her might.

It made him angry and he started towards her, but the other Indians laughed, and one who seemed to be the leader stopped him. Then with signs pointing to himself, his pony, and then with a sweep of his arm towards the west, he said, 'You go – me – be my squaw?'

Laura shook her head, and stamping her foot again, motioned them all to their ponies and away, telling them to go.

And they went, riding their running ponies without saddles or bridles.

But as they went their leader turned and looked back at Laura where she stood, with the wind blowing her skirts around her and her braids flying, watching them go away across the prairie into the west.

Wild geese were flying south. By day the sky was full of them flying in their V-formations, the leaders calling and their followers answering until the world seemed full of their calls. Even at night they could be heard as their seemingly endless numbers sailed ahead of the cold coming down out of the north.

Laura loved to watch them high against the blue of the sky, large V's and smaller V's with the leader at the point, his followers streaming behind, always in perfect V-formation. She loved to hear their loud, clear honk, honk. There was something so wild and free about it, especially at night when the lonely, wild cry sounded through the darkness, calling, calling. It was almost irresistible. It made Laura long for wings so that she might follow.

Manly said, 'The old saying is that "everything is lovely when the geese honk high", but I believe we will have a hard winter, the geese are flying so high and in such a hurry. They are not stopping to rest on the lakes nor to feed. They are hurrying ahead of a storm.' For several days, the wild geese hurried southward; and then one still, sunny afternoon a dark cloud line lay low on the north-west horizon. It climbed swiftly, higher and higher, until the sun was suddenly overcast, and with a howl the wind came and the world was blotted out in a blur of whirling snow.

Laura was in the house alone when the wind struck the north-west corner with such force the whole house jarred. Quickly she ran to the window but she could see only a wall of whiteness beyond the glass. Manly was in the barn, and at the sudden shriek of the storm he, too, looked out a window. Then, although it was only mid-afternoon, he fed the horses and cows for the night, milked the heifer in the little pail in which he had taken out some salt, and shutting the barn door carefully and tightly behind him, started for the house. As soon as he was away from the shelter of the hay at the barn door, the full force of the storm struck him. It seemed to come from every direction at once. Whichever way he turned his head he faced the wind. He knew the direction in which the house lay but he could see nothing of it. He could see nothing but a blur of white. It had grown intensely cold and the snow was a powdered dust of ice that filled his eyes and ears, and since he must breathe he felt smothered. After taking a few steps he could not see the barn. He was alone in a whirling white world.

Keeping his face in the right direction, Manly went ahead; but soon he knew he had gone far enough to be at the house, yet he could not see it. A few steps more and he stumbled against an old wagon that had been left some little distance south of the house. In spite of his guarding against it, the wind had blown him south of his way, but now he knew where he was. So again setting his face in the right direction he went on. Again he knew he should have reached the house but he had not. If he should become hopelessly confused he might not find it at all but wander out on the open prairie to perish, or he might even freeze within a few feet of the house before the storm was over. No shout of his could be heard above the wind. Well, he might as well go on a little farther, no use standing still. Another step, and his shoulder just lightly brushed something. He put up his hand and touched the corner of a building. The house! He had almost missed it and headed out into the storm.

Keeping his hand on the wall he followed it and came to the back door.

Blown in with the storm, as he opened the door, he stood and blinked the snow from his eyes in the warmth and shelter of the house he had so nearly missed. He still clutched the milk pail. In the struggle with the storm he had not spilled the milk – because it was frozen.

For three days and nights the blizzard raged. Before Manly went to the barn again, he followed the house wall to where the long rope clothesline was tied at the corner. With his hand on the rope, he followed it to the back of the house. Unfastening it at the corner, he followed the house around to the door and fastened the rope there, and to the loose end he tied a shorter rope, the drying line he had put up in the storm shed. Now unreeling the rope as he went he could go to the haystack at the barn door, make the rope fast, and follow it back to the house safely. After that he went to the barn and cared for the stock once a day.

While the blizzard shrieked and howled and raged outside, Laura and Manly both stayed indoors. Laura kept the fire going from the store of coal in the storm shed. She cooked from the stores in her pantry and cellar and she sang at her knitting in the afternoon. Old Shep and the cat lay companionably on the rug before the cook-stove and there was warmth and comfort in the little house standing so sturdily in the midst of the raging elements.

Late in the afternoon of the fourth day the wind went down. It lost its whirling force and blew the loose snow scudding close to the ground, packing it into hard drifts that lay over the prairie with bare ground showing between. The sun shone again with a frosty light and huge sundogs stood guard on each side of it. And it was *cold*! Laura and Manly went outdoors and looked over the desolate landscape. Their ears still throbbed to the tumult of the storm, and the silence following it was somehow confusing.

'This has been very bad,' Manly said. 'We will hear of plenty of damage from this.' Laura looked at the smoke rising from the stovepipe in their neighbour's house across the road. She had not been able to see it for three days. 'Larsens are all right anyway,' she said.

Next day Manly drove to town to get a few supplies and to learn the news.

The house was bright and cheerful when he came home. The last rays of the afternoon sun were shining in at the south window, and Laura was ready to help him off with his coat as he came in from the barn after putting up his team and doing the night feeding.

But Manly was very sober. After they ate supper he told Laura the news.

A man south of town, caught at his barn by the storm as Manly had been, had missed the house going back. He had wandered out on the prairie and had been found frozen to death when the wind went down.

Three children going home from school had become lost, but found a haystack and dug into it. They had huddled together for warmth and had been drifted in. When the storm stopped, the oldest, a boy, had dug out through the snow, and searchers had found them. They were weak from hunger but not frozen.

Range cattle had drifted before the storm for a hundred miles. Blinded and confused they had gone over a high bank of the Cottonwood River, the later ones falling on top of the first, breaking through the ice of the river and floundering in the water and loose snow until they had smothered and frozen to death. Men were dragging them out of the river now, hundreds of them, and skinning them to save the hides. Anyone who had lost cattle could go look at the brands and claim his own.

The storm so early in the season was unexpected, and many people had been caught out in the snow and had frozen hands and feet. Another storm came soon, but people were prepared now and no damage was done.

It was too cold for horseback riding, and snow covered the ground, so Manly hitched the driving team to the cutter (the little one-seated sleigh) on Sunday afternoons. Then he and Laura drove here and there, over to Pa's farm to see the home folks or to the Boasts, old friends who lived several miles to the east. But the drives were always short ones; no twenty or forty miles now. It was too dangerous, for a storm might come up suddenly and catch them away from home.

Barnum and Skip were not working now. They were fat and frisky and enjoyed the sleigh rides as much as Laura and Manly. They pranced and danced purposely to make their sleigh bells ring more merrily while their ears twitched alertly and their eyes shone.

Trixy and Fly, the saddle ponies, Kate and Bill, the working team, were growing fat in the barn and took their exercise in the haystack-sheltered barnyard at the back.

The holidays were near and something must be done about them. The Boast and the Ingalls families had spent them together whenever they could. Thanksgiving dinner at Boasts', Christmas dinner at the Ingalls' home. Now with Laura and Manly, there was a new family, and it was agreed to add another gathering to those two holidays. New Year's should be celebrated at the Wilders'.

Christmas presents were hardly to be thought of, the way the crops had turned out, but Manly made handsleds for Laura's little sisters, and they would buy Christmas candy for all.

For themselves, they decided to buy a present together, something they could both use and enjoy. After much studying of Montgomery Ward's catalogue, they chose to get a set of glassware. They needed it for the table and there was such a pretty set advertised, a sugar bowl, spoon-holder, butter dish, six sauce dishes, and a large oval-shaped bread plate. On the bread plate raised in the glass were heads of wheat and some lettering which read 'Give us this day our daily bread'.

When the box came from Chicago a few days before Christmas and was unpacked, they were both delighted with their present.

The holidays were soon over and in February Laura's nineteenth birthday came. Manly's twenty-ninth birthday was just a week later so they made one celebration for both on the Sunday between.

It wasn't much of a celebration, just a large birthday cake for two of them, and a little extra pains were taken in the cooking and arranging of the simple meal of bread, meat, and vegetables.

Laura had become quite a good cook and an expert in the making of light bread.

With work and play, in sunshine and storm, the winter passed. There was very little visiting or having company, for neighbours were rather far away (except for the Larsens across the road) and the days were short. Still, Laura was never lonely. She loved her little house and the housework. There were always Shep and the cat, and a visit to the horses and cows at the barn was, she thought, as good as visiting people any day.

When Trixy lipped her hand or rested her soft nose on her shoulder, or Skip, the scamp, searched her pocket for a lump of sugar, she felt that they were very satisfactory friends.

The wild geese were coming back from the south-land. They flew overhead from one lake to the other, where they rested on the water and fed along the shores.

The ground was bare of snow, and although the nights were cold and the wind often chilly, the sunshine was warm and spring had come. Manly was getting his ploughs and harrows in order for working the land to be ready for the sowing of wheat and oats. He must get an early start at the work for there were a hundred acres to sow in wheat and a fifty-acre oatfield on the homestead. At the shanty on the homestead Laura held the grain sacks while he shovelled the wheat into them. He was hauling them to the home barn to be handy for the sowing. The shanty was cold. The grain sacks were coarse and rough to the touch and the wheat was dusty.

Watching the plump wheat kernels slide into the open mouth of the sack made Laura dizzy. If she took her eyes from them, they were drawn irresistibly to the newspapers pasted on the shanty walls and she read the words over and over. She was unreasonably annoyed because some of them were bottom side up but she must read them anyway. She couldn't take her eyes from them. Words! Words! The world was full of words and sliding wheat kernels!

And then she heard Manly saying, 'Sit down a minute! You're tired.'

So she sat down, but she was not tired. She was sick. The next morning she felt much worse and Manly got his own breakfast.

For days she fainted whenever she left her bed. The doctor told her to lie quietly. He assured her she would feel much better before long and that in a few months, nine to be exact, she would be quite all right. Laura was going to have a baby.

So that was it! Well, she mustn't shirk. She must get around and do the work in the house so that Manly could get the crops in. So much depended on this year's crops, and there was no money to hire help.

Soon Laura was creeping around the house, doing what must be done, and whenever possible relieving her dizzy head by lying down for a few minutes. The little house grew to look rather dingy for she couldn't give it the care it had always had. As she went so miserably about her work she would smile wryly now and then as she remembered a saying of her mother's: 'They that dance must pay the fiddler.' Well, she was paying, but she would do the work. She *would* help that much in spite of everything.

The trees were not growing very well. The dry weather of the summer had been hard on them, and they must be given extra care, for years from now there must be the ten acres with the right numbers of growing trees in order to prove up on the tree claim and get a title to the land.

So Manly ploughed around the little trees and then mulched them with manure from the barnyard.

Laura missed the drives over the greening prairie in the freshness of early spring. She missed the wild violets that scented the air with their fragrance, but when wild rose time came in June she was able to ride behind Skip and Barnum along the country roads where the prairie roses on their low bushes made glowing masses of colour from pale pink to deepest red and the air was full of their sweetness. On one such drive she asked abruptly out of a silence, 'What shall we name the child?'

'We can't name it now,' Manly replied, 'for we don't know if it will be a boy or a girl.'

And after another silence Laura said, 'It will be a girl and we will call her Rose.'

It rained often that spring. It rained through the summer and the little trees took courage and waved their little green leaves in the wind while they stretched taller every day. The wild blue stem grass grew on the high prairie, and the slough grass grew rank in the sloughs where water stood in the lowest places.

And, oh, how the wheat and oats did grow! For it rained!

The days went by and by and the wheat headed tall and strong and green and beautiful. Then the grain was in the milk and in just a few days the crop would be safe. Even if it turned dry now there would be a good crop, for the stalks would ripen the wheat.

At last one day Manly came in from the field. He had been looking it over and decided it was ready to cut.

The wheat, he said, was perfect. It would go all of forty bushels to the acre and be Number One hard. The price would start at seventy-five cents a bushel delivered at the elevator in town.

'Didn't I tell you,' he said, 'that everything evens up? The rich have their ice in the summer, but the poor get theirs in the winter.' He laughed and Laura laughed with him. It was wonderful.

In the morning Manly had to go to town and buy a new

binder to harvest the wheat. He had waited until he was sure there would be a good crop before buying it, for it was expensive: two hundred dollars. But he would pay half after the grain was threshed and the other half in a second payment after threshing next year. He would only have to pay eight per cent interest on the deferred payment, and could give a chattel mortgage on the machine and cows to secure the debt. Manly went early to town; he wanted to be back in time to begin cutting the grain.

Laura was proud when Manly drove into the yard with the new machine. She went out and watched while he hitched on the four horses and started for the oatfield. The oats were ripest and he would cut them first.

As Laura went back into the house she did a little mental arithmetic – one hundred acres at forty bushels to an acre would be four thousand bushels of wheat. Four thousand bushels of wheat at seventy-five cents a bushel would be – Oh, how much would it be? She'd get her pencil. Four thousand bushels at seventy-five cents a bushel would be three thousand dollars. It couldn't be! Yes, that was right! Why, they would be rich! She'd say the poor *did* get their ice!

They could pay for the mowing machine and the hayrake Manly had bought a year ago and could not pay for because the crop had been so poor. The notes of seventy-five dollars and forty dollars and the chattel mortgage on Skip and Barnum would be due after threshing. Laura did not mind the notes so much, but she hated the chattel mortgage on the horses. She'd almost as soon have had a mortgage on Manly. Well, it would soon be paid now, *and* the note for the sulky plough with its chattel mortgage on the cows. She thought there were some store accounts but was not sure. They couldn't be much anyway. Perhaps she could have someone to do the work until the baby came. Then she could rest: she needed rest, for, not being able to retain her food for more than a few minutes, she had not much to live on and was very emaciated. It would be nice to let someone else do the cooking. The smell of cooking always made her feel so nauseated now.

Manly cut the fifty acres of oats with the new McCormick binder that day. He was jubilant at night. It was a wonderful crop of oats and early tomorrow he would begin on the wheat.

But, the next morning, when Manly had cut twice around the wheatfield, he unhitched and came back to the barn with the team. The wheat would be better for standing a couple of days longer. When he came to cut it, it was not quite so ripe as he had thought, and he would take no chance of shrunken kernels by its being cut a little green, Manly said. But it was even heavier than he had figured, and if it didn't go above forty bushels to the acre, he was mistaken. Laura felt impatient. She was in a hurry for the wheat to be cut and safely stacked. From the window she could see the shining binder standing at the edge of the grain and it looked impatient too, she thought.

After noon that day the DeVoes came by. Cora stopped to spend some time while her husband Walter went on to town. The DeVoes were about the same age as Manly and Laura and had been married about as long. Laura and Cora were very good friends and it was a pleasant afternoon except for being rather uncomfortable from the heat.

As the afternoon passed it grew hotter and there was no wind, which was unusual. It left one gasping for breath and feeling smothered.

About three o'clock Manly came in from the barn and said it was going to rain for sure. He was glad he had not been cutting the wheat to have it lie in a rainstorm before he could get it shocked. The sunshine darkened, and the wind sighed and then fell again as it grew darker yet. Then the wind rose a little, and it grew lighter, but the light was a greenish colour. Then the storm came. It rained only a little; then hailstones began to fall, at first scattering slowly, then falling thicker and faster while the stones were larger, some of them as large as hens' eggs.

Manly and Cora watched from the windows. They could not see far into the rain and the hail, but they saw Ole Larsen, across the road, come to his door and step out. Then they saw him fall, and someone reached out the door, took hold of his feet, and dragged him in. Then the door shut.

'The fool,' Manly said, 'he got a hailstone on the head.'

In just twenty minutes the storm was over, and when they could see as far as the field, the binder was still there but the wheat was lying flat. 'It's got the wheat, I guess,' Manly said. But Laura could not speak.

Then Manly went across the road to find what had happened to Mr Larsen. When he came back, in a few minutes, he said that Mr Larsen had stepped out to pick up a hailstone so large that he wished to measure it. Just as he stooped to pick it up, another one hit him on the head. He was unconscious for several minutes after he was dragged in by the heels, but was all right now except for a sore head.

'And now let's make some ice cream,' Manly said. 'You stir it up, Laura, and I'll gather up hailstones for ice to freeze it.'

Laura turned to Cora where she stood speechless, looking out of the window. 'Do you feel like celebrating, Cora?' she asked.

And Cora answered, 'No! I want to get home and see what has happened there. Ice cream would choke me!'

The storm had lasted only twenty minutes but it left a desolate, rain-drenched and hail-battered world. Unscreened windows were broken and bent. The ground was covered with hailstones so thickly, it looked covered with a sheet of ice, and they even lay in drifts here and there. Leaves and branches were stripped off the young trees and the sun shone with a feeble, watery light over the wreck. The wreck, thought Laura, of a year's work, of hopes and plans of ease and pleasure. Well, there would be no threshers to cook for. Laura had dreaded the threshing. As Ma used to say, 'There is no great loss without some small gain.' That she should think of so small a gain bothered Laura.

She and Cora sat white and silent until Walter drove up to the door, helped Cora into the wagon, and drove away almost forgetting to say good-bye in their anxiety to get home and learn how bad the storm had been there.

Manly went out to look at the wheatfield and came in sober enough. 'There is no wheat to cut,' he said. 'It is all threshed and pounded into the ground. Three thousand dollars' worth of wheat planted, and it's the wrong time of the year.'

Laura was muttering to herself, 'The poor man gets his –'

'What's that?' Manly asked.

'I was only saying,' Laura answered, 'that the poor man got his ice in the summer this time.'

At two o'clock the next day hailstones were still lying in drifts in low places.

Though plans are wrecked, the pieces must be gathered up and put together again in some shape. Winter was coming. Coal must be bought to last through. That would cost between sixty and one hundred dollars. Seed grain would have to be bought for next spring's sowing. There were notes on the machinery coming due.

There was the binder that had been used to cut only fifty acres of oats; there was the sulky plough and the mower and rake, the seeder that had sown the grain in the spring and the new wagon. There was too the five hundred dollars still due on the building of the house. 'Five hundred dollars' debt on the house!' Laura exclaimed. 'Oh, I didn't know that!'

'No,' Manly said. 'I didn't think there was any need to bother you about that.'

But something must be done about all this, and he would go

to town tomorrow and see what could be done. Perhaps he could raise money with a mortgage on the homestead. That was proved up on, thank goodness. He couldn't give a mortgage on the tree claim. That belonged to Uncle Sam until Manly had raised those trees. And Laura thought she could hear her father singing, 'Our Uncle Sam is rich enough to give us all a farm!' Sometimes Laura was afraid her head was a little flighty, but that extra five hundred dollars' debt had been something of a shock. Five hundred and two hundred was seven hundred, and the wagon and the mower ... She must stop counting it or she would have her head queer.

Manly found he could renew all his machinery notes for a year by paying the interest. He could even make the first payment on the binder after the next harvest, postponing the second payment to the year after. He could sell all the wild hay he had for four dollars a ton delivered at the railroad in town. Buyers wanted it to ship to Chicago.

But he could not raise money with a mortgage on the homestead unless they were living on it. He must have money to pay the interest due, for living expenses and for seed. There was no way to get the money except by moving to the homestead. If they were living on the homestead he could mortgage it for eight hundred dollars.

A newcomer would buy Kate and Bill for more than Manly had paid for them. Manly would not need them, for he had found a renter for the tree claim on shares; Manly would furnish the seed.

Skip and Barnum, with Trixy and Fly to do the driving, could do the work on the one place.

If someone else worked the tree claim, Manly could raise more crops on the homestead and have more profit from the farms than if he tried to work both claims all by himself.

An addition would have to be built on the homestead claim shanty before they moved but they could do with one new room and a cellar underneath through using the original shanty for a storeroom.

So it was decided. Manly hurried to stack the oats, which the hail had threshed to the ground, but the oat straw made good animal feed to take the place of hay and that would leave more hay to sell.

When the oats were hauled to the homestead and stacked, Manly dug the hole in the ground for the cellar, and over it built the one-room addition to the claim shanty. Then he built the frame of a barn, cut slough hay, and when it was dry stacked it around the frame to make a hay barn.

Everything was ready now for the moving. Manly and Laura moved to the homestead the next day after the barn was finished.

It was the twenty-fiith of August. And the winter and the summer were the first year.

2. The Second Year

It was a beautiful day, that twenty-fifth of August, 1886, when Manly and Laura moved to the homestead.

'A fine day, as fine as our wedding day just a year ago, and it's a new start just as that was. And a new home, if it is some smaller.

'We'll be all right now. You'll see! "Everything evens up in the end. The rich man –"'

His voice trailed silent but Laura couldn't help finishing the Irishman's saying to herself: 'The rich man has his ice in the summer and the poor man gets his in the winter.' Well, they had got theirs in that hailstorm and in the summer too.

But she mustn't think about that now. The thing to do was to get things arranged in the new home and make it cheerful for Manly. Poor Manly, he was having a hard time and doing his very best. The house wasn't so bad. The one new room was narrow (twelve feet by sixteen) and not very long, facing the south with a door and a window on a narrow porch, closed at the west end by the old claim shanty.

There was a window in the east end of the room. The looking glass was hung beside it in the south corner and the parlour table stood under it. The head of the bed came close to the window on the other side and extended along the north wall.

The kitchen stove was in the north-west corner of the room and a kitchen cupboard stood beside it. The kitchen-dining table stood against the west wall close to the south end.

The carpet from the old bedroom was across the east end of

the room, and the armchair and Laura's little rocking chair stood on it, close to each other between the windows. The sun came in through the east window in the mornings and shone across the room. It was all very snug and pleasant.

The room that had been the claim shanty was convenient as a storage room, and the stock were comfortable in their new barn. Sheltered from the north and west by the low hill and facing the south, it would be warm in winter.

The whole place was new and fresh. The wind waved the tall grass in the slough that stretched from the foot of the hill by the barn to the south and to the east line of the farm. The house was at the top of the low hill and there would always be grassland in front of it.. The ploughland lay to the north of the hill out of sight from the house. Laura was glad of that. She loved the sweep of unbroken prairie with the wild grasses waving in the winds. To be sure, that whole place was grassland now, except for a small field. Ten acres of cultivated land were required by law before proving up on a homestead. But the grass to the north of the house was upland, blue stem, and not the tall slough grass that grew so rankly in low places. It was haying time, and every day counted in the amount of hay that could be put up before winter.

Because of the hailstorm, hay would be the only crop this year. So as soon as breakfast was over the day after moving, Manly hitched Skip and Barnum to the mowing machine and began cutting hay.

Laura left her morning's work undone and went with him to see the work started, and then because the air was so fresh and the new-cut hay so clean and sweet, she wandered over the field, picking the wild sunflowers and Indian paintbrush. Presently she went slowly back to the house and her unfinished tasks.

She didn't want to stay in the house. There would be so much of that after the baby came. And she felt much better out in the fresh air. So after that she did as little as possible in the house, and instead stayed out in the hayfield with Manly.

When he loaded the hay in the big hayrack to haul to the barn, Laura, already in the wagon, stepped up on each forkful as it was pitched in and so gradually rose with the load until she was on the top, ready to ride to the barn. At the barn she slid down the hay into Manly's arms and was safely on the ground.

Manly made the stacks in the field with a bull rake. The bull rake was a long wide plank with long wooden teeth set in it at intervals for the whole length. A horse was hitched at each end, and, walking one on each side of a long windrow of hay, they pulled the plank sideways. The long teeth slipped under the hay and it piled up in front of the plank and was pushed along the ground.

When there was enough of a load and it was where the stack was to be, Manly tipped the plank. It went over the top of the hay which was left in a pile. Several of these piles started the stack. Then as the horses came to it, one went on each side of the stack, the rake went on up, Manly followed it and spilled the hay on top of the stack and then went down the other end after another load.

Barnum was good and always walked along with his end of the plank on his side of the stack. But Skip stopped when he had no driver, so Laura drove Skip the length of the stack and then sat against the sweet hay on the sunny side while Manly would bring up another load with the rake.

When the stack was high enough, Manly raked down the sides with his pitchfork and gathered up all the scattered hay around and against it, making all neat and even. Then he topped the stack with a load of hay from the wagon.

So the nice fall weather passed. Nights grew cooler, frost came. The haying was finished.

Manly had mortgaged the homestead for eight hundred

dollars, so now he could buy the coal for winter, and it was stored in the storeroom.

The taxes of sixty dollars (there were no taxes on the tree claim because they had no title yet) were paid. Interest, on the notes given for machinery, was paid. There was money for seed in the spring and to live on, they hoped, until next harvest.

The hay had helped. Manly had sold thirty tons at four dollars a ton, and the $120 was a year's income from the crops.

Wild geese were late coming from the north, and when they did, seemed in no hurry to go on south. Instead they fed in the sloughs and flew from one lake to the other, where the water was nearly covered with them as they swam about. The sky was filled with their V-shaped flocks and the air rang to their calls. Manly hurried into the house for his gun one day.

'A flock of geese is coming over so low, I believe I can get one,' he told Laura.

Quickly he went out the door, and forgetting that the old gun kicked, he held it up before his face, sighted and pulled the trigger.

Laura followed him just in time to see him whirl around with his hand to his face.

'Oh, did you hit a goose?' she asked.

'Yes, but I didn't quite kill it,' he answered, as he wiped the blood from his nose.

The flock of geese went on unharmed to join their kindred at the lake.

It was going to be an open winter; the geese knew there was no hurry to go south.

The small field was soon ploughed and the hurry of work was over.

In November, the snow came and covered the ground, making good sleighing. Manly and Laura, well bundled up and covered with robes, went often for sleigh rides on sunny afternoons. Because Laura felt so much better outdoors, Manly made a handsled and a breast-collar-harness for Old Shep.

On pleasant days Laura hitched Shep to the handsled and let him pull her on it down the hill to the road. Then together they would climb the hill, Shep pulling the sled and Laura walking beside him to take another ride down until she was tired from the walking and the fun. Shep never got tired of it and at times when the sled tipped against a drift and Laura rolled into the snow he seemed actually to laugh.

And so November passed and December came.

The sun was shining on the morning of the fifth of December, but it looked stormy in the north.

'Better play outdoors all you can today, for it may be too stormy tomorrow,' Manly said.

So, soon after breakfast Laura hitched Shep to the sled and took the day's first ride down the hill. But she stayed out only a little while.

'I don't feel like playing,' she told Manly when he came up from the barn. 'I would rather curl up by the stove.' And again after the dinner work was done she sat idly by the stove in her little rocking chair, which worried Manly.

Along in the afternoon Manly went to the barn and came back with the horses hitched to the sleigh.

'I'm going for your Ma,' he said. 'Keep as quiet as you can until we come.' It was snowing hard now as from the window Laura watched him drive down the road with the team trotting their best. She thought that the pace would have won them the prize at the Fourth of July races.

Then she walked the floor or sat by the stove until Manly came back with her Ma.

'My goodness,' Ma exclaimed, as she warmed herself by the fire. 'You should not be up. I'll get you to bed right away.'

49

And Laura answered, 'I'll have a long time to stay in bed. I am going to stay up now as long as I can.'

But soon she made no objections and only vaguely knew when Manly drove away again to fetch a friend of her Ma's from town.

Mrs Powers was a friendly, jolly Irish woman. The first Laura knew of her being there was hearing her say, 'Sure she'll be all right, for it's young she is. Nineteen you say; the very age of my Mary. But we'd better have the doctor out now, I'm thinking.' When Laura could again see and know what went on around her, Ma and Mrs Powers were standing one on each side of her bed. And was that Manly at the foot? No! Manly had gone for the doctor. Then were there two Ma's and two Mrs Powerses? They seemed to be all around her.

What was that old hymn Pa used to sing?

> ... angel bank
> Come and around me stand,
> Oh, bear me away on your snowy wings
> To –

She was being borne away on a wave of pain. A gust of cold, fresh air brought her back and she saw a tall man drop his snowy overcoat by the door and come towards her in the lamplight.

She vaguely felt a cloth touch her face and smelled a keen odour. Then she drifted away into a blessed darkness where there was no pain.

When Laura opened her eyes, the lamp was still shining brightly over the room, and Ma was bending over her with the doctor standing beside her. And in the bed by her side was a little warm bundle.

'See your little daughter, Laura! A beautiful baby, and she weighs just eight pounds,' Ma said.

'It's a fine girl you are yourself,' Mrs Powers said from where she was sitting by the fire. 'A fine, brave girl, and baby'll be good because of it. You'll be all right now.'

So Manly took the doctor and Mrs Powers home, but Ma stayed, and Laura went to sleep at once with her hand resting gently on little Rose.

Rose was such a good baby, so strong and healthy that Ma stayed only a few days. Then Hattie Johnson came. 'To wash baby this time, instead of windows,' she said.

But soon Hattie went and the three, Manly, Laura and Rose, were left by themselves in the little house atop the low hill with the sweep of the empty prairie all around it.

There was not a house near enough for neighbours, but a mile away across the slough a few buildings on the edge of town were in sight.

A hundred precious dollars had gone for doctor bills and medicine and help through the summer and winter so far; but after all, a Rose in December was much rarer than a rose in June, and must be paid for accordingly.

Christmas was at hand and Rose was a grand present. Then the day before Christmas Manly hauled a load of hay to town and brought back the most beautiful clock. It stood nearly two feet high from its solid walnut base to the carved leaf at its very top. The glass door that covered the face was wreathed with a gilt vine on which four gilt birds fluttered, and the pendulum that swung to and fro behind them was the colour of gold too.

The clock had such a pleasant, cheerful voice as it said tick, tock, and when it struck the hour its tone was clear and sweet. Laura loved it at once.

The old round, nickel alarm clock could not be depended on to tell the right time, but still it would have answered the need, and Laura said doubtfully, 'But ought you –' Then Manly told her he had traded the load of hay for it, and it would be a Christmas present for all three of them. The hay he had kept for feed was holding out so well that there would be more than enough to take the stock through the rest of the winter, and he couldn't have sold the load of hay for money because they were not shipping any more.

Christmas was a happy time even though it was a stormy day, and they stayed quietly at home.

After the Christmas storm the weather was clear and sunny but cold – twenty-five and thirty below zero on some days.

But one day seemed unusually warm and Laura had been at home so long, she wanted to go for a sleigh ride to see Ma and Pa. Could they take the baby out safely?

They were sure they could. Some blankets were put to warming by the stove. Manly drove the cutter close to the door and made a little warm nest of them in the shelter of the dashboard. Rose was wrapped in her own warm blankets and a little red cloak and hood, with a thin blue silk handkerchief lightly covering her face, and tucked tightly in among the blankets in the cutter.

Then away they went, the horses stepping quickly and the sleigh bells singing merrily.

Several times Laura put her hand in among the blankets and touched Rose's face to be sure that she was warm and that there was air beneath the veil.

It seemed only a few minutes until they drove up to the homeplace and went quickly into the house, where Ma and Pa both scolded them well.

'You're crazy!' Pa said. 'Out with that baby when it is fifteen below.' And so it was by the thermometer. 'She might have smothered,' Ma added.

'But I watched. She couldn't have,' Laura answered.

And Rose waggled her fingers and cooed. She was warm and happy and had had a good nap.

Laura had never thought it might be dangerous to take the

baby out, and she was anxious on the way home and glad when they were safely there. It seemed there was a good deal to taking care of babies.

There were no more sleigh rides for some time, and then one day that was really warm they drove the four miles to see their good friends, the Boasts.

Mr and Mrs Boast lived by themselves on their farm. They had no children and could hardly make fuss enough over Rose.

When at last the visit was over and Mr Boast was standing by the buggy to see them start, he started to speak, then hesitated and finally said in a queer voice, 'If you folks will let me take the baby in to Ellie for her to keep, you may take the best horse out of my stable there and lead it home.'

Manly and Laura were still in astonishment, and Mr Boast went on. 'You folks can have another baby and we can't. We never can.'

Manly gathered up the reins, and Laura said with a little gasp, 'Oh, no! No! Drive on, Manly!' As they drove away, she hugged Rose tightly; but she was sorry for Mr Boast as he stood still where they had left him, and for Mrs Boast waiting in the house, knowing, she was sure, what Mr Boast was going to propose to them.

The rest of the winter passed quickly. There were no more storms and the weather was warm for the season. April came and on all the farms seeding was begun.

On the twelfth of April, Manly went down to the barn to hitch up for the afternoon's work.

When he went into the barn the sun was shining warmly and he had no thought of storm. But when the horses were combed and brushed and harnessed, just as he was starting to take them out, there was a crash as of something smashing against the whole side of the barn. Then he heard the shriek of the wind and looking out could see nothing but whirling snow. A blizzard in April! Why, it was time for spring's work! Manly could hardly believe his eyes. He rubbed them and looked again. Then he unharnessed the team and went to the house. It was quite a little way to go and nothing whatever could be seen except the whirling snow, but there were things scattered along the path – the cutter, the wagon, the bobsled. Taking his direction from the way each stood as he came to it, he went on to the next and came safely to the porch and the house. Laura was anxiously trying to see from the window to the barn, hoping for a glimpse of Manly coming, but she couldn't see him until the door opened.

It was the worst storm of the winter and lasted two days, with no slacking of the wind which held steadily to its high wild shriek.

But all was snug at the house. The stock were safe and warm in the barn, and following the line of sleds and wagon, Manly managed to get safely to them and back once a day to give them water and fill the mangers.

When on the morning of the third day the sun rose bright and the wind came only in low gusts, it looked a wintry world. A good many people had been caught in the storm and two travellers nearby had lost their lives.

While Mr Bowers was working in his field, two miles south of town, two strangers had come walking from town. They stopped and inquired the way to Mr Mathews, saying they were friends of his from Illinois. Mr Bowers pointed out Mr Mathews' house to them, in plain sight across the prairie, and the strangers went on their way. Soon the storm struck and Mr Bowers went from the field to his buildings and shelter.

The day the storm was over, Mr Bowers saw Mr Mathews passing on his way to town and inquired about his friends from Illinois. Mr Mathews had not seen them, so the two went searching for them.

The two strange men were found in a haystack that stood

by itself on the open prairie, considerably off the course they should have followed. They had pulled hay out of the stack and lighted it to make a fire. Then they evidently had given up the idea of keeping warm by an open fire in the wind and snow and had crawled into the hole in the haystack. There they had frozen to death.

If they had kept walking, they could have 'walked out' the storm, for it lasted only two days. Or if they had been properly dressed, they would not have frozen inside the haystack. But their clothes were thin, for springtime in Illinois, and not for a western blizzard.

The snow was soon gone again, and spring really came, with the singing of meadow larks and the sweetness of violets and new grass as all the prairie turned a beautiful soft green.

Laura put Rose in a clothes-basket with her tiny sunbonnet on her head and set the basket nearby while she and Manly planted the garden.

The old dog Shep was gone. He never had become reconciled to Rose but always was jealous of her. One day he went away and never came back, and his fate was never known. But a friendly, stray Saint Bernard, a huge, black dog, had come to the house and been adopted in Shep's place.

The Saint Bernard seemed to think his special job was to watch over Rose, and wherever she was, there he would be curled around her or sitting up close again·t her.

The cook-stove was moved into the store-room, leaving the other room cooler for the hot weather, and in the summer kitchen Laura worked happily, with Rose and the big, black dog playing or sleeping on the floor.

There could be no horseback riding safely with a baby, but Laura did not miss it so much, because Manly fastened a dry-goods box in the front of the road-cart, leaving just enough room for Laura's feet at the end where the driver sat. When the work was done after dinner, Laura would hitch Barnum to the road-cart and with Rose in her pink sunbonnet sitting in the box would drive away wherever she cared to go. Sometimes just to town, but more often to see her Ma and the girls.

At first Ma was afraid to have Rose travel that way, but soon she became used to it. Although Barnum was a fast driver, he was as gentle as a kitten, and the cart on its two wheels was light and safe. Rose could not fall out of the box, and Laura was a good driver. She never had a moment's uneasiness with Barnum hitched to the road-cart.

And Manly didn't care how often she went, just so she came home in time to get supper.

With housework, garden work, caring for and driving with Rose, the summer soon passed and it was haying time again. Now Rose sat in the shelter of a windrow of hay and watched while Laura drove Skip on the bull rake.

Laura and Manly both liked to stay out in the sunny hayfield, and leaving Rose asleep with the big dog watching over her, Laura sometimes drove Skip and Barnum on the mowing machine while Manly raked hay with Fly and Trixy.

There were no threshers to cook for this fall, for the renters on the tree claim had the threshing done.

The yield of grain was not nearly so much as it should have been. The season had been too dry. And the price of wheat was lower – only fifty cents a bushel.

Still there was money enough to pay all the interest and some of the smaller notes, those for the mowing machine and horse rake and for the sulky plough, and the first payment was made on the harvester. There were still the wagon note and the five hundred dollars due on the house and the eight-hundred-dollar mortgage on the homestead. Seed must be kept for the next sowing, taxes must be paid, the coal must be bought, and they must live until after the next harvest.

There would also be the hay again, and this year there were

two steers to sell. They were nice large two-year-olds, and they would sell for twelve dollars each; twenty-four dollars would help buy groceries.

They hadn't done so badly, considering the season.

The twenty-fifth of August had come again, and this winter and summer were the second year.

3. The Third Year

With the coming of cool weather, Laura proposed moving the cook-stove back into the bed-sitting room, and she could not understand why Manly put it off, until one day when he came from town with a hard-coal heater.

It was a beautiful stove, the black iron nicely polished and all the nickel trimmings shining brightly.

Manly explained how buying the stove would be a saving in the end. It would take so little coal to keep it going that even though the price per ton was twelve dollars instead of the soft coal price of six, the cost would be less. Then there would be a steady, even heat night as well as day. It would keep them from taking cold by being first warm and then chilly, as with the cook-stove. The nickel top of the new stove was movable and all the cooking except baking could be done on it. On baking days a fire could be made in the summer kitchen.

Rose was creeping, or rather hitching herself, around on the floor these days, and the floor must be kept warm for her.

Laura felt that they couldn't afford the beautiful new stove, but that was Manly's business. She need not bother about it – and he did suffer with the cold. It seemed as though he could never get clothes warm enough. She was knitting him a whole long-sleeved undershirt of fine, soft, Shetland wool yarn for a Christmas surprise.

It was difficult to keep it hidden from him and get it finished, but after Christmas she could knit its mate easily.

Manly wore the new shirt when they drove in the cutter to eat Christmas dinner with the home folks.

It was dark when they started for home again and it had begun to snow. Luckily it was not a blizzard but only a snowstorm and, of course, a wind. Rose was warmly wrapped and sheltered in Laura's arms, with blankets and robes wrapped around them both and Manly in his fur coat beside them.

The going was slow against the storm in the darkness and after some time Manly stopped the horses. 'I believe they're off the road. They don't like to face the wind,' he said.

He unwrapped himself from the robes, climbed out of the cutter, and looked closely at the ground, trying to find the tracks of the road, but the snow had covered every sign of it. But finally by scraping away the snow with his feet, he found the wheel tracks of the road underneath and only a little to one side.

So Manly walked the rest of the way, keeping to the road by the faint signs of it that he could find now and then, while all around in the darkness was falling snow and empty open prairie.

They were thankful when they reached home and the warmth of the hard-coal baseburner. And Manly said his new undershirt had proven its worth.

Though the weather was cold, there were no bad blizzards and the winter was slipping by very pleasantly. Laura's Cousin Peter had come up from the southern part of the state and was working for the Whiteheads, neighbours who lived several miles to the north. He often came to see them on Sunday.

To surprise Manly on his birthday Laura asked Peter and the Whiteheads to dinner, cooking and baking in the summer kitchen. It was a pleasant day and warm for winter and the dinner was a great success.

But in spite of the warm day Laura caught a severe cold and had a touch of fever so that she must stay in bed. Ma came over to see how she was and took Rose home with her for a few days. Instead of getting better, the cold got worse and settled in Laura's throat. The doctor when he came said it was not a cold at all but a bad case of diphtheria.

Well, at least Rose was out of it and safe with Ma, if she had not taken it with her. But there were several anxious days, while Manly cared for Laura, until the doctor reported that Rose had escaped the disease.

But then Manly came down with it, and on his morning visit, the doctor ordered him to bed with strict orders to stay there. He said he would send someone out from town to help them. A short time after the doctor went away, Manly's brother Royal came out to care for them. He was a bachelor, living alone, and thought he was the one could best come.

So both in the same room, with the crudest care, Manly and Laura spent the miserable, feverish days. Laura's attack had been dangerous, while Manly's was light.

At last they were both up and around again, but the doctor had given his last advice and warning against over-exertion. Royal, tired and half sick himself, had gone home, and Laura and Manly, well wrapped, had spent a day in the summer kitchen while the sick room was fumigated.

Then after a few days longer, Rose was brought home. She had learned to walk while she had been away and she seemed to have grown much older. But it was very pleasant to have her taking her little running steps around the room, and most of all, it was good to be well again.

Laura thought the trouble was all over now. But that was not to be for many a day yet.

Manly – disregarding the doctor's warning – had worked too hard, and one cold morning he nearly fell as he got out of bed, because he could not use his legs properly. They were numb to his hips and it was only after much rubbing that he could get about with Laura's help.

But together they did the chores; after breakfast, Laura helped him hitch up the wagon and he went to town to see the doctor.

'A slight stroke of paralysis,' the doctor said, 'from over-exertion too soon after the diphtheria.'

From that day on there was a struggle to keep Manly's legs so that he could use them. Some days they were better and again they were worse, but gradually they improved until he could go about his usual business if he was careful.

In the meantime spring had come. Sickness with its doctor bills had been expensive. There was no money to go on until another harvest. The renter on the tree claim was moving away and Manly in his condition could not work both pieces of land. The tree claim was not proved up and the young trees must be cultivated to hold it.

Something must be done. And in this emergency a buyer for the homestead came along. He would assume the eight-hundred-dollar mortgage and give Manly two hundred. And so the homestead was sold and Manly and Laura moved back to the tree claim one early spring day.

The little house was in bad order, but a little paint, a few fly screens, and a good cleaning made it fresh and sweet again. Laura felt that she was back home, and it was easier for Manly to walk on the level ground to the barn than it had been for him to climb up and down the hill on the homestead.

He was gradually overcoming the effect of the stroke but still would fall down if he happened to stub his toe. He could not step over a piece of board in his way but must go around it. His fingers were clumsy so that he could neither hitch up nor unhitch his team, but he could drive them once they were ready to go.

So Laura hitched up the horses and helped him get started and then was on hand ready to help him unhitch when he drove them back.

The renter had taken the tree claim with the fall ploughing done so he turned it back to Manly ploughed. Manly had only to harrow and seed the fields. It was slow work but he finished in good time.

The rains came as needed and the wheat and oats grew well. If it would only keep on raining often – and not hail.

There were three little calves in the barn lot and two young colts running all over the place, plus the colt they had bought with Laura's school money, now a three-year-old and grown out nicely. The little flock of hens were laying nicely. Oh, things weren't so bad after all.

Rose was toddling about the house, playing with the kitten or clinging to Laura's skirts as she went about the work.

It was a busy summer for Laura, what with the housework, caring for Rose, and helping Manly whenever he needed her. But she didn't mind doing it all, for Manly was recovering the use of his hands and feet.

Slowly the paralysis was wearing off. He was spending a great deal of time working among the young trees. It had been too dry for them to grow well the summer before and they were not starting as they should this spring.

Some of them had died. The dead ones Manly replaced, setting the new ones carefully. He pruned them all, dug around their roots, and then ploughed all the ground between.

And the wheat and oats grew rank and green.

'We'll be all right this year,' Manly said. 'One good crop will straighten us out and there never was a better prospect.'

The horses were not working hard now. Skip and Barnum did what was necessary and the ponies, Trixy and Fly, were growing fat on their picket ropes. Manly said they should be ridden, but Laura could not leave Rose alone; neither could she take her during the day with safety and pleasure.

It was quiet and there was nothing to do after supper when Rose was put to bed. She was so tired with her play that she slept soundly for hours. So Laura and Manly came to saddling the ponies and riding them on the road before the house, on the run for a half mile south and back, then around the half-circle drive before the house, a pause to see that Rose was still sleeping, and a half mile north and back for another look at Rose until ponies and riders were both ready to stop. Trixy and Fly enjoyed the races they ran in the moonlight and the shying at the shadow of a bunch of hay in the road or the quick jump of a jack rabbit across it.

Cousin Peter came one Sunday to tell Manly and Laura that Mr Whitehead wanted to sell his sheep, a hundred pure-bred Shropshires.

A presidential election was coming in the fall and it looked as though the Democrats were due to win. If they did, Mr Whitehead, being a good Republican, was sure the country would be ruined. The tariff would be taken off, and wool and sheep would be worth nothing. Peter was sure they could be bought at a bargain. He would buy them himself if only he had a place to keep them. 'How much of a bargain? What would you have to pay?' Manly asked.

Peter was sure he could buy them for two dollars apiece since Mr Whitehead was feeling particularly uneasy about the election. 'And the sale of their wool next spring ought nearly to pay for them,' he added. There were one hundred sheep. Peter had one hundred dollars due him in wages. That would be half of the money needed to buy them at two dollars each. Laura was thinking aloud. They had land enough by using the school section that lay just south of them: a whole section of land with good grazing and hay free to whoever got there first and used it. For the first time Laura was glad of the Dakota law that gave two sections in every township to the schools. And especially glad that one of them adjoined their tree claim.

'We'd have pasture and hay enough and we could build good shelter,' Manly said.

'But the other one hundred dollars?' Laura asked doubtfully.

Manly reminded her of the colt that they had bought with her school money, and said he believed he could sell it now for one hundred dollars. She could buy half the sheep if she wanted to gamble on them.

And so it was decided. If Peter could get the sheep for two hundred, Laura would pay half. Peter was to care for the sheep, herding them on the school section in summer. Together Peter and Manly would put up the hay, with Manly furnishing teams and machinery. Back of the hay barn they would build on another one for the sheep, opening onto a yard fenced with wire. Peter would live with them and help with the chores in return.

A few days after the colt was sold, Peter came driving the sheep into the yard that had been built for them. There were a hundred good ewes and six old ones that had been thrown in for nothing.

Every morning after that, Peter drove the sheep out onto the school section to graze, carefully herding them away from the grass that would be mowed for hay.

The rains came frequently. It even seemed as though the winds did not blow as hard as usual, and the wheat and oats grew splendidly.

The days hurried along towards harvest. Just a little longer now and all would be well with the crop.

Fearful of hail, Manly and Laura watched the clouds. If only it would not hail.

As the days passed bringing no hailstorm, Laura found herself thinking. Everything will even up in the end; the rich have their ice in the summer but the poor get theirs in the winter. When she caught herself at it, she would laugh with a nervous catch in her throat. She must not allow herself to be under such a strain. But if only they could harvest and sell this crop, it would mean so much. Just to be free of debt and have the interest money to use for themselves would make everything so much easier through the winter that was coming soon.

At last the wheat was in the milk and again Manly estimated that the yield would be forty bushels to the acre. Then one morning the wind blew strong from the south and it was a warm wind. Before noon the wind was hot and blowing harder. And for three days the hot wind blew.

When it died down at last and the morning of the fourth was still, the wheat was dried and yellow. The grains were cooked in the milk, all dried and shrunken, absolutely shrivelled. It was not worth harvesting as wheat but Manly hitched Skip and Barnum to the mowing machine and mowed it and the oats, to be stacked like hay and fed without threshing to the stock as a substitute for both hay and grain.

As soon as this was done, haying was begun, for they must cut the hay on the school section ahead of anyone else. It was theirs if they were the first to claim and cut it. Laura and Rose went to the hayfield again. Laura drove the mower while Manly raked the hay cut the afternoon before. And a neighbour boy was hired to herd the sheep while Peter helped Manly stack the hay. They stacked great ricks of hay all around the sheep barn and on three sides of the sheep yard, leaving the yard open on the south side only.

And the twenty-fifth of August came and passed and the third year of farming was ended.

4. A Year of Grace

Fall ploughing was begun as soon as haying was finished, but the work was too hard for Skip and Barnum to do even with the help of the ponies. Trixy and Fly were small and could not pull with strength. They were intended only for riding. Fly objected strenuously at times, kicking savagely when her tugs were being hitched.

Once when Laura was helping Manly hitch the horses to the plough and keeping watch of Rose at the same time, she lost sight of Rose. Immediately she stopped working with the harness, and looking quickly around the yard, said, 'Manly, where is Rose?'

And a little hand pulled Fly's tail away from her body, on the opposite side of the four horses abreast, a little face showed between Fly and her tail, and Rose's little voice said, 'Here I am!'

Now Manly's hands were not nearly so stiff and clumsy. Perhaps he could soon hitch the straps and buckle the buckles himself.

The team was tired at night. Laura could hardly bear to see them at the unhitching, Skip with his gay head hanging and Barnum's dancing feet standing so patiently still.

Manly said he would have to get another team, for he wanted to break the sixty acres of sod and have the whole 160 acres ready to seed in the spring.

'But the three years are up. So you call this farming a success?' Laura objected.

'Well, I don't know,' Manly answered. 'It is not so bad. Of course, the crops have been mostly failures, but we have four cows now and some calves. We have the four horses and the colts and machinery and there are the sheep ... If we could only get one crop. Just one good crop, and we'd be all right. Let's try it one more year. Next year may be a good crop year and we are all fixed for farming now, with no money to start anything else.'

It sounded reasonable as Manly put it. There didn't seem to be anything else they could do, but as for being all fixed – the five hundred dollars still due on the house worried Laura. Nothing had been paid on it. The binder was not yet paid for and interest payments were hard to make. But still Manly might be right. This might be when their luck turned, and one good year would even things up.

Manly bought two Durham oxen that had been broken to work. They were huge animals. King was red and weighed two thousand pounds. Duke was red-and-white spotted and weighed twenty-five hundred pounds. They were as gentle as cows, and Laura soon helped hitch them up without any fear – but she fastened Rose in the house while she did so. They were cheap: only twenty-five dollars each and very strong. Now Skip and Barnum took the ponies' place and did the light work, while the cattle hitched beside them drew most of the load.

The ploughing was finished easily and the breaking of the sod was done before the ground froze. It was late in doing so for it was a warm pleasant fall.

The winter was unusually free of bad blizzards, though the weather was very cold and there was some snow.

The house was snug and comfortable with storm windows and doors, and the hard-coal heater in the front room between the front door and the east window. Manly had made the storm shed, or summer kitchen, tight by battening closely all the cracks between the board sheeting, and the cook-stove had been left there for the winter. The table had been put in its place in the front room between the pantry and bedroom doors, and Peter's cot-bed stood against the west wall of the room where the table used to stand. Geraniums blossomed in tin cans on the window sills, growing luxuriantly in the winter sunshine and the warmth from the hard-coal heater.

The days passed busily and pleasantly. Laura's time was fully occupied with her housework and Rose, while Rose was an earnest, busy little girl with her picture books and letter blocks and the cat, running around the house, intent on her small affairs.

Manly and Peter spent much of their time at the barn, caring for the stock. The barn was long, from the first stalls where the horses and colts stood, past the oxen, King and Duke, the cows and the young cattle, the snug corner where the chickens roosted, on into the sheep barn where the sheep all ran loose.

It was no small job to clean out the barn and fill all the mangers with hay. Then there was the grain to feed to the horses, and they had to be brushed regularly. And all the animals must be watered once a day.

On pleasant days Manly and Peter hauled hay in from the stacks in the fields and fed the animals from that, leaving some on the wagon in the sheep-yard for the sheep to help themselves.

This was usually finished well before chore time, but one afternoon they were delayed in starting. Because the snow drifts were deep, they were hauling hay with King and Duke. The oxen could go through deep snow more easily than horses, but they were slower, and darkness came while Manly and Peter were still a mile from home.

It had begun to snow: not a blizzard, but snow was falling thickly in a slow, straight wind. There was no danger, but it was uncomfortable and annoying to be driving cattle, wallowing through snow in the pitch dark and the storm.

Then they heard a wolf howl and another; then several together. Wolves had not been doing any damage recently and there were not so many left in the country, but still they were seen at times, and now and then they killed a stray yearling or tried to get into a flock of sheep.

'That sounds toward home and as though they were going in that direction,' Manly said. 'Do you suppose they will go into the sheep-yard?'

'Not with Laura there,' Peter answered. But Manly was not so sure and they tried to hurry faster on their way.

At home Laura was beginning to be anxious. Supper was nearly ready, but she knew Manly and Peter would do the night chores before they ate. They should have been home before now and she wondered what could have happened.

Rose had been given her supper and was sleeping soundly, but Nero, the big, black dog, was uneasy. Now and then he raised his head and growled.

Then Laura heard it – the howl of a wolf! Again the wolf howled, and then several together, and after that, silence.

Laura's heart stood still. Were the wolves coming to the sheep-yard? She waited, listening, but could hear nothing but the swish of the snow against the windows; or was that a sheep bleating?

Must she go to the sheep-yard and see that they were all right? She hesitated and looked at Rose, but Rose was still asleep. She would be all right if left alone. Then Laura put on her coat and hood, lighted the lantern, and taking it and the dog with her, went out into the darkness and the storm.

Quickly she went to the stable door, opened it, and reaching inside secured the five-tined stable fork; then shutting the door again, she went the length of the barn, flashing her lantern light as far as she could in every direction.

Nero trotted ahead of her, sniffing the air. Around the sheep-yard they went but everything was quiet except for the sheep moving restlessly around inside. There was no sight nor sound of the wolves until, as Laura stood by the yard gate listening for the last time before going back to the house, there came again the lone cry of a wolf. But it was much farther to the north than before. The wolves had gone by on the west and all was well, though Nero growled low in his throat. Laura hadn't known she was frightened until she was safely in the house; then she found her knees trembling and sat down quickly.

Rose was still asleep and it was not long before Manly and Peter were there.

'What would you have done if you had found the wolves?' Manly asked.

'Why, driven them away, of course. That's what I took the pitchfork for,' Laura answered.

In December Laura felt again the familiar sickness. The house felt close and hot and she was miserable. But the others must be kept warm and fed. The work must go on, and she was the one who must do it.

On a day when she was particularly blue and unhappy, the neighbour to the west, a bachelor living alone, stopped as he was driving by and brought a partly filled grain sack to the house. When Laura opened the door, Mr Sheldon stepped inside, and taking the sack by the bottom, poured the contents out on the floor. It was a paper-backed set of Waverley novels.

'Thought they might amuse you,' he said. 'Don't be in a hurry! Take your time reading them!' And as Laura exclaimed in delight, Mr Sheldon opened the door, closed it behind him quickly, and was gone. And now the four walls of the close, overheated house opened wide, and Laura wandered with brave knights and ladies fair beside the lakes and streams of Scotland or in castles and towers, in noble halls or lady's bower, all through the enchanting pages of Sir Walter Scott's novels.

She forgot to feel ill at the sight or smell of food, in her hurry to be done with the cooking and follow her thoughts back into the book. When the books were all read and Laura came back to reality, she found herself feeling much better.

It was a long way from the scenes of Scott's glamorous old tales to the little house on the bleak, wintry prairie, but Laura brought back from them some of their magic and music and the rest of the winter passed quite comfortably.

Spring came early and warm. By the first of April a good deal of seeding had been done and men were busy in all the fields. The morning of the second was sunny and warm and still. Peter took the sheep out to graze on the school section as usual, while Manly went to the field. It was still difficult for him to hitch up the team, and Laura helped him get started. Then she went about her morning's work.

Soon a wind started blowing from the north-west, gently at first but increasing in strength until at nine o'clock the dust was blowing in the field so thickly that Manly could not see to follow the seeder marks. So he came from the field and Laura helped him unhitch and get the team in the barn.

Once more in the house they could only listen to the rising wind and wonder why Peter didn't bring the sheep in. 'He couldn't have taken them far in such a short time and he surely would bring them back,' Manly said. Dust from the fields was blowing in clouds so dense that they could see only a little way from the windows, and in a few minutes Manly went to find Peter and the sheep and help if help were needed.

He met Peter with the sheep about four hundred yards or one-quarter of a mile from the barn. Peter was on foot, leading his pony and carrying three lambs in his arms. He and the dog were working the sheep towards their yard. The sheep could hardly go against the wind but they had to face it to get home. They had not been sheared and their fleeces were long and heavy. The poor sheep with their small bodies and little feet carrying such a load of fluffy wool caught too much wind. If a sheep turned ever so little sideways, the wind would catch under the wool, lift the sheep from its feet and roll it over and over, sometimes five or six times before it could stop. Against the strength of the wind it was impossible for the sheep to get to its feet. Peter would lift it up and stand it on its feet headed right so it could walk into the wind. He was tired and the sheep dog and pony were powerless to help, so it was time for Manly to be there.

It took them both over an hour to get all the sheep the four hundred yards and into the yard.

After that they all sat in the house and let the wind blow. Their ears were filled with the roar of it. Their eyes and throats smarted from the dust that was settling over the room even though the doors and windows were tightly closed.

Just before noon there came a knock at the door, and when Manly opened it, a man stood on the step.

'Just stopped to tell you, your wheels are going round,' he said, and with a wave of his hand towards the barn, he ran to his wagon, climbed in, and drove on down the road. His face was black with dust and he was gone before they recognized him as the man who had bought their homestead.

Laura laughed hysterically. 'Your wheels are going round,' she said. 'What did he mean?' She and Manly went into the kitchen and looked from the window towards the barn and then they knew. Between the house and barn, the hay wagon with the big hayrack on it had been left standing. The wind had lifted it, turned it over and dropped it bottom side up. The wagon rested on the rack underneath, leaving the wheels free in the air, and every one of the four wheels was turning in the wind.

There was only a cold bite to eat at noon for no one felt like eating and it was not safe to light a fire.

About one o'clock Laura insisted that she could smell fire and that there must be a prairie fire near, but no smoke could be seen through the clouds of dust.

The wind always rises with a fire, and on the prairie the wind many times blows strongly enough to carry flame from the fire to light grass ahead of the burning, so that the fire travels faster than the grass burns. Once Manly and Peter had raced towards a fire trying to save a large haystack that stood between it and them. They ran their horses' heads up to the stack and jumped off just as a blown flame lit the opposite end of the haystack. Each had a wet grain sack to fight the fire. They scrambled up the stack and slid down the end, scraping the fire off and putting it out at the ground after it had burned back a little way from the end of the stack. They let it run down each side as a back fire and the main fire raced by and on, leaving the haystack with Manly and Peter and horses untouched. The horses had stood with their heads against the stack where they could breathe.

The wind reached its peak about two o'clock, then slackened gradually, so slowly at first it was hardly noticeable, but it died away as the sun went down and was still.

Rose lay asleep with her tired, dusty little face streaked with perspiration. Laura felt prostrated with exhaustion, and Manly and Peter walked like old men as they went out to the barn to see that the stock was all right for the night.

Later they learned that there had been a prairie fire during the sixty-five miles an hour wind, a terrible raging fire that hardly hesitated at firebreaks, for the wind tore flames loose and carried them far ahead of the burning grass. In places the fire leaped, leaving unburned prairie, the flame going ahead and the wind blowing out the slower fire in the grass as a candle is blown out.

Houses and barns with good firebreaks around them were burned. Stock was caught and burned. At one place a new lumberwagon stood in a ploughed field a hundred yards from the grass. It was loaded with seed wheat just as the owner had left it when he had gone from the field because of the wind. When he went back there was nothing left of the wagon and its load except the wagon irons. Everything else had burned.

There was no stopping such a fire and no fighting it in such a wind.

It went across the country, leaving a blackened prairie behind until it reached the river, and then the wind went down with the sun. There it stopped, somewhere between fifty and one hundred miles from where it began.

There was nothing to do but to re-seed the fields, for the seed was blown away or buried in the drifts of soil around the edges of the ploughed land.

So Manly bought more seed wheat and oats at the elevator in town, and at last the seeding was finished.

Then the sheep were sheared and the selling of the wool cheered them all, for wool was worth twenty-five cents a pound and the sheep averaged ten pounds of wool apiece. Each sheep had paid for itself and fifty cents more with its wool alone. By the last of May, the lambs had all arrived, and there were so many twins that the flock was more than doubled. Lambing time was a busy time, both day and night, for the sheep must be watched and the lambs cared for. Among the hundred sheep there were only five ewes who could not or would not care for their lambs. These five lambs were brought into the house and warmed and fed milk from a bottle and must be raised by hand.

Rose spent her time playing in the yard now, and Laura tried to watch her as the little pink sunbonnet went busily bobbing here and there.

Once Laura was just in time to see Rose struggle upright in

the tub of water that stood under the pump spout; and with water running down her face and from her spread fingers at each side, Rose said without a whimper, 'I want to go to bed.'

One afternoon, just after Rose had been washed and combed and dressed in fresh, clean clothes, Laura heard her shrieking with laughter, and going to the door, saw her running from the barn. 'O-o-o,' Rose called. 'Barnum did just like this.' And down she dropped in the dusty path, and with arms and legs waving, rolled over and over on the ground. She was such a comical sight that Laura could only laugh too, in spite of the wreck of the clean dress, the dirt on her face and hands and the dust in her hair.

Another time, Laura missed her from the yard and with fear in her heart ran to the barn door. Barnum was lying down in his stall and Rose sat on his side, kicking her heels against his stomach.

Carefully, so as not to disturb his body, the horse raised his head and looked at Laura and she was positive Barnum winked one eye.

After that Laura tried to watch Rose closer, but she couldn't bear to keep her in the house with the spring so fresh and gay outside. The work must be done between moments of looking at Rose through door and window.

Once again she was just in time to see Rose miss an accident by a narrow margin. She had evidently gone farther afield than usual and was just coming back around the corner of the barn. Then Kelpie, Trixy's latest colt, came running around the same corner with another colt chasing her. Kelpie saw Rose too late to turn, too late to stop, so she put an extra spring in her muscles and sailed over Rose's head, while Susan, the other colt, proving, as she always tried to, that she could do anything Kelpie did, followed behind, going neatly over Rose's head.

Then Laura was there, and snatching Rose up, carried her to the house. Rose had not been frightened, but Laura was, and she felt rather sick. How could she ever keep up the daily work and still go through what was ahead. There was so much to be done and only herself to do it. She hated the farm and the stock and the smelly lambs, the cooking of food and the dirty dishes. Oh, she hated it all, and especially the debts that must be paid whether she could work or not.

But Rose *hadn't* been hurt and now she was wanting a bottle to feed one of the pet lambs. Laura would do the same; she'd be darned if she'd go down and stay down or howl about it. What was it someone had said in that story she read the other day? 'The wheel goes round and round and the fly on the top'll be the fly on the bottom after a while.' Well, she didn't care what became of the top fly, but she did wish the bottom one could crawl up a little way. She was tired of waiting for the wheel to turn. And the farmers were the ones at the bottom, she didn't care what Manly said. If the weather wasn't right they had nothing, but whether they had anything or not they must find it somehow to pay interest and taxes and a profit to the businessmen in the town on everything they bought, and they must buy to live. There was that note at the bank Manly had to give to get the money to buy the grain for the re-seeding after the wind storm. He was paying three per cent a month on that note. That was where the wool money would have to go. No one could pay such interest as that. But there was all the summer's living before another harvest. Her head spun when she tried to figure it out.

Would there be enough money to pay it? Their share of the wool money was only $125, and how much was that note? A bushel to the acre of seed wheat and $1 a bushel for the seed: $100. Sixty acres of oats and two bushels to the acre of seed: 120 bushels. At 42¢ a bushel, that would be $50.40. Added to the $100 for wheat the note must be for $150.40.

It seemed to make a great difference in the price whether they were selling wheat or buying it. To be sure, as Manly said, there were freight charges out and back and elevator charges. But it didn't seem fair even so.

Anyway, they should pay the note at the bank as soon as possible. If they had to do so they could buy a book of coupons at the grocery store and give a note for that at only two per cent a month. It was rather nice that the merchants had got those books with coupons from 25¢ to $5 in twenty-five or fifty-dollar books. It was convenient and it was cheaper interest. They had not bought any yet, and she had hoped they would not have to. Somehow the thought of it hurt her pride worse than a note at the bank. But pride must not stand in the way of a saving of one per cent. She wouldn't think about it any more. Manly would do as he thought best about it. It was his business and he wasn't worrying.

As spring turned the corner into summer, the rains stopped and the grain began to suffer for lack of moisture. Every morning Manly looked anxiously for signs of rain, and seeing none, went on about his work.

And then the hot winds came. Every day the wind blew strongly from the south. It felt on Laura's cheek like the hot air from the oven when she opened the oven door on baking day. For a week, the hot winds blew, and when they stopped, the young wheat and oats were dried, brown and dead.

The trees on the ten acres were nearly all killed too. Manly decided there was no hope of replanting to have the trees growing to fulfil the law for the claims.

It was time to prove up and he could not. There was only one way to save the land. He could file on it as a pre-emption. If he did that he must prove up in six months and pay the United States $1.25 an acre. The continuous residence would be no trouble, for they were already there. The two hundred dollars cash at the end of the six months would be hard to find, but there was no other way. If Manly did not file on the land someone else would, for if he failed to prove up, the land would revert to the Government and be open to settlement by anyone.

So Manly pre-empted the land. There was one advantage: Manly did not have to work among the trees any more. Here and there one had survived and those Manly mulched with manure and straw from the barn. The mulching would help to keep the land moist underneath and so help the trees to live. The cottonwood tree before Laura's pantry window, being north of the house, had been protected from the full force of the hot winds and from the sun. It was growing in spite of the drought. Laura loved all its green branches that waved just the other side of the glass as she prepared food on the broad shelf before the window and washed the dishes there.

No rain followed the windstorm, but often after that cyclone clouds would form in the sky and then drift away. It was cyclone weather.

One sultry afternoon, Manly was in town and Peter gone with the sheep. Laura finished her work and she and Rose went out in the yard. Rose was playing with her dishes under the cottonwood tree on the shady side of the house while Laura idly watched the clouds more from force of habit than a real fear, for she had become used to the danger of storms.

The wind had been from the south strongly in the morning, but had died down, and now Laura noticed clouds piling up in the north. There was a solid bank of blackness and before it clouds rolled. Now the wind rose, blowing hard from the south, and watching, Laura saw the dreaded funnel-shaped cloud drop its point towards the ground from the wall of black. The light turned a greenish colour, and seizing Rose, Laura ran with her into the house. She quickly shut all the doors and windows before she ran into the pantry to look again, from its window, towards the storm.

The point of the funnel had touched the ground and she could see the dust rise up. It passed over a field of new breaking and the strips of sod were lifted up out of sight. Then it struck an old haystack. There was a blur and the stack disappeared. The funnel-shaped cloud was moving towards the house. Laura lifted the trap door in the pantry floor and taking Rose with her went quickly through it into the cellar, dropping the door shut behind her. Holding Rose tightly, she cowered close in a corner in the darkness and listened to the wind shriek above them, expecting every second that the house would be lifted and carried away.

But nothing happened, and after what seemed hours but was really only a few minutes she heard Manly's voice calling.

Lifting the cellar door Laura carried Rose up the stairs. She found Manly standing by his team in the yard, watching the storm as it passed eastward less than a quarter of a mile north from where they stood. It went on blowing away buildings and haystacks, but only a sprinkle of rain fell on the parched earth. Manly, in town, had seen the storm cloud and hurried home so that Laura and Rose should not be alone.

There were no more cyclones, but the weather continued hot and dry, and August the fifth was especially warm.

In the afternoon Manly sent Peter to bring Laura's Ma, and at four o'clock he sent Peter again to town, this time on his running pony for the doctor. But their son was born before the doctor could get there.

Laura was proud of the baby, but strangely she wanted Rose more than anything. Rose had been kept away from her mother for the sake of quiet, and a hired girl was taking in-different care of her. When Laura insisted, the girl brought Rose in, a shy little thing with a round baby face herself, to see the little brother.

After that Laura rested easily and soon could take an interest in the sounds from outside, knowing well, from them, what was going on.

One day Peter came to the bedroom door to bid her good morning. He had stuck a long feather in his hatband and as it nodded above his good-natured face he looked so comical that Laura had to laugh.

Then she heard him talking to his pony and calling his dog and knew he was taking the sheep out. He was singing:

> Oh, my! but ain't she handsome!
> Dear me! she's the sweetest name!
> Ky! yi! to love her is my dooty,
> My pretty, little, posy-pink
> Jenny Jerusha Jane.

And Peter and the sheep were gone until night.

Then she heard Rose playing with the pet lambs. They were so large now that three of them went out with the sheep, but the two smallest still hung around the back door and yard to be fed and played with. Often they pushed Rose over, but it was all in the game. Then she heard the hired girl refuse to give Rose a piece of bread and butter, speaking crossly to her, and that Laura could not bear. Calling from her bed, she settled the question in Rose's favour.

Laura felt she must hurry and get her strength back. Rose shouldn't be meanly treated by any hired girl; and besides, there were the wages of five dollars a week. They must be stopped as soon as possible for the time would come soon enough to pay a note.

Laura was doing her own work again one day three weeks later when the baby was taken with spasms, and he died so quickly that the doctor was too late.

To Laura, the days that followed were mercifully blurred. Her feelings were numbed and she only wanted to rest – to rest and not to think.

But the work must go on. Haying had begun and Manly, Peter, and the herd boy must be fed. Rose must be cared for and all the numberless little chores attended to.

The hay was going to be short of what was needed, for it had been so dry that even the wild prairie grass had not grown well. There were more sheep and cattle and horses to feed, so there must be more hay instead of less.

Manly and Peter were putting up hay on some land two miles away a week later. Laura started the fire for supper in the kitchen stove. The summer fuel was old, tough, long, slough hay, and Manly had brought an armful into the kitchen and put it down near the stove.

After lighting the fire and putting the tea kettle on, Laura went back into the other part of the house, shutting the kitchen door.

When she opened it again, a few minutes later, the whole inside of the kitchen was ablaze: the ceiling, the hay, and the floor underneath and wall behind.

As usual, a strong wind was blowing from the south, and by the time the neighbours arrived to help, the whole house was in flames.

Manly and Peter had seen the fire and come on the run with the team and the load of hay.

Laura had thrown one bucket of water on the fire in the hay, and then, knowing she was not strong enough to work the pump for more water, taking the little deed-box from the bedroom and Rose by the hand, she ran out and dropped on the ground in the little half-circle drive before the house. Burying her face on her knees she screamed and sobbed, saying over and over, 'Oh, what will Manly say to me?' And there Manly found her and Rose, just as the house roof was falling in.

The neighbours had done what they could but the fire was so fierce that they were unable to go into the house.

Mr Sheldon had gone in through the pantry window and thrown all the dishes out through it towards the trunk of the little cottonwood tree, so the silver wedding knives and forks and spoons rolled up in their wrappers had survived. Nothing else had been saved from the fire except the deed-box, a few work clothes, three sauce dishes from the first Christmas, and the oval glass bread plate around the margin of which were the words, 'Give us this day our daily bread'.

And the young cottonwood stood by the open cellar hole, scorched and blackened and dead.

After the fire Laura and Rose stayed at her Pa's for a few days. The top of Laura's head had been blistered from the fire and something was wrong with her eyes. The doctor said the heat had injured the nerves and so she rested for a little at her old home, but at the end of the week Manly came for her.

Mr Sheldon needed a housekeeper and gave Laura and Manly houseroom and use of his furniture in return for board for himself and his brother. Now Laura was so busy she had no time for worry, caring for her family of three men, Peter, and Rose, through the rest of the haying and while Manly and Peter built a long shanty, three rooms in a row, near the ruins of their house. It was built of only one thickness of boards and tar-papered on the outside, but it was built tightly, and being new, it was very snug and quite warm.

September nights were growing cool when the new house was ready and moved into. The twenty-fifth of August had passed unnoticed and the year of grace was ended.

Was farming a success?

'Well, it all depends on how you look at it,' Manly said when Laura asked him the question.

They had had a lot of bad luck, but anyone was liable to have bad luck even if he weren't a farmer. There had been so many dry seasons now that surely next year would be a good crop year.

They had a lot of stock. The two oldest colts would be ready to sell in the spring. Some newcomer to the land would be sure to want them, and there were the younger colts coming on. There were a couple of steers ready to sell now. Oh, they'd likely bring twelve or thirteen dollars apiece.

And there were the sheep, twice as many as last year to keep, and some lambs and the six old sheep to sell.

By building the new house so cheaply, they had money left to help pay for proving up on the land.

Maybe sheep was the answer. 'Everything will be all right, for it all evens up in time. You'll see,' Manly said, as he started for the barn.

As Laura watched him go, she thought, yes, everything is evened up in time. The rich have their ice in the summer, but the poor get theirs in the winter, and ours is coming soon.

Winter was coming on, and in sight of the ruins of their comfortable little house they were making a fresh start with nothing. Their possessions would no more than balance their debts, if that. If they could find the two hundred dollars to prove up, the land would be theirs, anyway, and Manly thought he could.

It would be a fight to win out in this business of farming, but strangely she felt her spirit rising for the struggle.

The incurable optimism of the farmer who throws his seed on the ground every spring, betting it and his time against the elements, seemed inextricably to blend with the creed of her pioneer forefathers that 'it is better farther on' – only instead of farther on in space, it was farther on in time, over the horizon of the years ahead instead of the far horizon of the west.

She was still the pioneer girl and she could understand Manly's love of the land through its appeal to herself.

'Oh, well,' Laura sighed, summing up her idea of the situation in a saying of her Ma's, 'we'll always be farmers, for what is bred in the bone *will* come out in the flesh.'

And then Laura smiled, for Manly was coming from the barn and he was singing:

> You talk of the mines of Australia,
> They've wealth in red gold, without doubt;
> But, ah! there is gold in the farm, boys –
> If only you'll shovel it out.

1889-1894

The first four years were over. Manly and Laura, with their small daughter Rose, stayed on in Dakota Territory for another five years. Then, in 1894, they decided to leave drought-stricken Dakota and to make a fresh beginning in the Ozark Hills, in Missouri, 650 miles to the south-east.

They travelled to Missouri in a covered wagon, and Laura kept a diary describing the journey. Many years later this was published under the title On the Way Home. Her daughter Rose wrote a setting for the book, telling how Laura and Manly left De Smet, Dakota, behind them, and came to Mansfield, Missouri, to make a new home: Rocky Ridge Farm, where they were to live happily all the rest of their long lives together.

In that setting Rose describes how things were in De Smet in 1894, when Laura and Manly decided to set out on the long journey to the south –

Epilogue

By Rose Wilder Lane
from *On the Way Home*

1 De Smet, Dakota

For seven years there had been too little rain. The prairies were dust. Day after day, summer after summer, the scorching winds blew the dust and the sun was brassy in a yellow sky. Crop after crop failed. Again and again the barren land must be mortgaged, for taxes and food and next year's seed. The agony of hope ended when there was no harvest and no more credit, no money to pay interest and taxes; the banker took the land. Then the bank failed.

In the seventh year a mysterious catastrophe was worldwide. All banks failed. From coast to coast the factories shut down, and business ceased. This was a Panic.

It was not a depression. The year was 1893, when no one had heard of depressions. Everyone knew about Panics; there had been Panics in 1797, 1820, 1835, 1857, 1873. A Panic was nothing new to Grandpa, he had seen them before; this one was no worse than usual, he said, and nothing like as bad as the wartime. Now we were all safe in our beds, nobody was rampaging but Coxey's Armies.

All the way from California Coxey's Armies of Unemployed were seizing the railroad trains, jam-packing the cars and running them full speed, open throttle, hell-for-leather towards Washington. They came roaring into the towns, yelling 'Justice for the Working Man!' and stopped and swarmed out, demanding plenty to eat and three days' rations to take with them, or they'd burn the town. People gave them everything to get rid of them. In all the cities Federal troops were guarding the Government's buildings.

I was seven years old and in the Second Reader at school but I had read the Third Reader and the Fourth, and Robinson Crusoe and Gulliver's Travels. The Chicago Inter-Ocean came every week and after the grown-ups had read it, I did. I did not understand all of it, but I read it.

It said that east of the Miss-Issippi there were no trains on the railroad tracks. The dis-patchers had dis-patched every train to the far-away East to keep them safe from Coxey's Armies. So now the Armies were dis-banded and walking on foot towards Washington, robbing and raiding and stealing and begging for food as they went.

For a long time I had been living with Grandpa and Grandma and the aunts in De Smet because nobody knew what would become of my father and mother. Only God knew. They had diff-theer-eeah; a hard word and dreadful. I did not know what it was exactly, only that it was big and black and it meant that I might never see my father and mother again.

Then my father, man-like, would not listen to reason and stay in bed. Grandma almost scolded about that, to the aunts. Bound and determined to get out and take care of the stock, he was. And for working too hard too soon, he was 'stricken'. Now he would be bedridden all his days, and what would Laura do? With me on her hands, besides.

But when I saw my father again he was walking, slowly. He limped through the rest of his ninety years and was never as strong as he had been.

We lived then in our own house in De Smet, away from Main Street, where only a footpath went through the short brown grasses. It was a big rented house and empty. Upstairs and down it was dark and full of stealthy little sounds at night, but then the lamp was lighted in the kitchen, where we lived. Our cookstove and table and chairs were there; the bed was in an empty room and at bedtime my trundle bed was brought into the warmth from the cookstove. We were camping, my mother said; wasn't it fun? I knew she wanted me to say yes, so I did. To me, everything was simply what it was.

I was going to school while my father and mother worked. Reading, writing, spelling, arithmetic, penmanship filled days almost unbearably happy with achievements satisfying Miss Barrows's strict standards. 'Procrastination is the thief of time,' I wrote twenty times in my penmanship book, without error or blot; and 'Evil communications corrupt good manners,' and 'Sweet are the uses of adversity,' every t and d exactly twice as tall as a vowel and every l exactly three times as tall; every t crossed; every i dotted.

All the way home down the long board walk in late afternoons we diligent scholars warmly remembered our adored Miss Barrows's grave, 'Well done', and often we sang a rollicking song. It was the song of those days heard more often than Ta-ra-ra boom-de-ay. My aunt Grace, a jolly big girl, often sang it, sometimes my mother did, and nearly all the time you could hear some man or boy whistling it.

> O Dakota land, sweet Dakota land,
> As on thy burning soil I stand
> And look away across the plains
> I wonder why it never rains,
> Till Gabriel blows his trumpet sound
> And says the rain has gone around.
> We don't live here, we only stay
> 'Cause we're too poor to get away.

My mother did not *have* to go out to work; she was married, my father was the provider. He got a day's work here and there; he could drive a team, he could carpenter, or paint, or spell a storekeeper at dinner-time, and once he was on a jury, downtown. My mother and I slept at Grandma's then, every night; the jury was kept under lock and key and my father could not come home. But he got his keep and two dollars every day for five straight weeks and he brought back all that money.

My mother worked to save. She sewed at the dressmaker's from six o'clock to six o'clock every day but Sunday and then came home to get supper. I had peeled the potatoes thin and set the table. I was not allowed to touch the stove. One day my mother made sixty good firm buttonholes in one hour, sixty minutes; nobody else could work so well, so fast. And every day, six days a week, she earned a dollar.

We were going to The Land of the Big Red Apple when we had enough money. Someone named Mr Sherwin had gone there and seen it, so the pictures that he sent back were true: pictures of huge red apples and rows of much smaller trees, and of buildings confusingly named Mansfield. They were not a man's field, and the print under them said they were The Gem City of the Ozarks.

Around and under these pictures on beautifully shiny paper I read that The Gem City of the Ozarks was in The Land of the Big Red Apple in Missouri. Now I knew three Miss States: Miss-issippi, Miss-consin, and Miss-ouri. Paul said, scornfully, that it wasn't Miss-consin, it was *Wis*-consin, but Wis didn't make sense to me.

Paul and George Cooley were coming with us to The Land of the Big Red Apple. Paul was oldest, George was next, I was only the youngest but they had to let me boss because I was a girl. We had always known each other. Their father had two big teams and two big covered wagons, and Paul would be allowed to drive one of them; he said his father said he could. I did not want to believe this but I knew that Paul would never lie. He was a big boy, too, going on ten years old.

My mother had saved one hundred dollars to take to The Land of the Big Red Apple. All those dollars were one piece of paper, named 'a hundred dollar bill'. She hid it in her writing desk, a fascinating wooden box which my father had made and polished so shiny-smooth that stroking it was rapture. It opened on little brass hinges to lie spread flat and be a slanting green felt surface to write on. At the top was a darling wooden tray to hold my mother's pearl-handled pen, and beside this was an inkwell. And the green felt was on a lid that lifted up on tinier hinges to reveal the place for writing paper, underneath it. I was allowed to see and touch the desk only when my mother opened it.

The hundred dollar bill was a secret. My mother locked it in the desk. Mr and Mrs Cooley knew, perhaps Paul and George did, but we must not talk about it. I must never, never, speak one word about that hundred dollar bill, not to anyone. Never, no matter what happened.

In the shade of the big empty house my father painted our covered wagon. It was really better than a covered wagon; it had been a two-seated hack though now it had only the front seat. My father painted it shiny black. He made a flat top for it, of black oilcloth, and put straight curtains of the black oilcloth on both sides and the back. Each curtain would roll up when he pulled a rope. Behind the seat he fitted the bedsprings and my mother made up the bed on them. At night she would make my bed on the floor in front of the seat.

She baked two dozen hardtacks for the journey. They were as large as a plate, flat and hard. Being so hard and dry, they would not spoil as bread would. It was a hard tack to gnaw, but it tasted almost like a cracker.

We were going to make haste, driving every day to reach The Land of the Big Red Apple and get settled before winter. We could not stop to look for work, but we would need more food on the way, so my father bought a box of asbestos firemats to trade, or to sell for ten cents apiece.

Fire-mats were a new thing, unheard-of. They looked like round pieces of grey-white pasteboard edged with a narrow strip of tin. Nobody could believe that they would not burn, till my father proved it. He would urge doubters to make a hot fire, hotter and hotter, then he laid one of those mats right into the flames. It would glow red and watchers would jeer, but that mat came out unharmed. Put one of those fire-mats under a pot, my father would say, and the pot could boil bone-dry, not a potato in it would so much as scorch. Every woman alive needed one of those mats.

Everything that we were taking all the way was packed under the bedsprings first. Next, the things that we would be using: the table and chairs with folding legs and the sheet-iron camp-stove that my father had made; the hammock that blind Aunt Mary had netted and given to us as a parting present; the writing desk, well wrapped; plates, cups, frying pan, coffee pot, wash basin, water pail, picket ropes and pegs; the hard-tack in its box. My father tied down the back curtain. Outside it he fastened the hencoop while the hens fluttered and squawked inside the wire netting. But they would soon be used to travelling.

In the next morning we said goodbye to Grandpa and Grandma, to the aunts Mary and Carrie and Grace, who all stood around to watch us go, though Aunt Mary's beautiful eyes could not see us. The mares were hitched to the hack; their colts, Little Pet and Prince, would follow them. The Cooleys' covered wagons had gone ahead, and Paul was driving the second one. I climbed up over our wagon's wheel and onto the seat by myself. My mother sat beside me; beside her my father tightened the lines; everyone said, 'Goodbye, goodbye!' 'Don't forget to write. I won't, I will, you be sure to. Good-bye!' and we drove away.

Away from Grandma's house with its rag-carpets and rocking-chair, the hymn books on the organ, my very own footstool; away from the chalky schoolroom where angelic Miss Barrows taught Kindergarten, Primer, First and Second

Readers; away from the summer sidewalks where grasshoppers hopped in the dry grass and the silver-lined poplar leaves rattled overhead; away from the gaunt grey empty house, and from Mrs Sherwood and her sister who sometimes on sweltering afternoons asked me to fetch ten cents' worth of ice cream from the far-away ice cream parlour, and shared it with me; away from De Smet to The Land of the Big Red Apple.

DE SMET

SOUTH DAKOTA

MISSOURI R.

Sioux City

NEBRASKA

PLATTE R.

Lincoln

IOWA

N
W E
S

MISSOURI

MISSOURI R.

Topeka

Kansas City

KANSAS

OZARK PLATEAU

Springfield

MANSFIELD

The 650 mile Journey
De Smet, Dakota to Mansfield, Missouri
made by Laura, Manly and Rose
July 17 – August 30, 1894

July 17 - August 30, 1894

Laura, Manly and Rose left De Smet, Dakota, on July 17, 1894. They travelled across Nebraska and Kansas, and crossed into Missouri on August 22. Three days later they were among the Ozark hills, in beautiful wooded country. This was a land of many clear, clean springs and streams. The farther they drove, the more they liked it. 'The sky seems lower here,' wrote Laura in her diary, 'and it is the softest blue. The distances and the valleys are blue whenever you can see them. It is a drowsy country that makes you feel wide awake and alive but somehow contented.'

They came into Mansfield, Missouri, on August 30, in a long line of other wagons. The map on page 96 shows the route they took on that long journey – over 650 miles.

Mansfield was a good town of about three hundred and fifty inhabitants. It had churches, stores, a bank, a blacksmith's shop, a flour mill, and a school for Rose. A railroad ran along one side of the square, and there were two stage coach lines, one running north, the other south.

'There is everything here already that one could want,' wrote Laura, and went on, 'Camped in the woods in the western edge of town and this afternoon Manly looked over one place for sale but was not exactly suited.' Rose wrote –

11 Mansfield, Missouri

I do not remember how many days my father spent hunting for land that the secret hundred dollar bill would buy. Every morning he rode away with some land agent to limp up and down the hills and to come back at evening, nothing found yet.

Paul and George and I were joyous. After the long boredom and so many dull days that we hardly remembered De Smet, now every day was Sunday without Sunday's clean clothes and staid behaviour. The camp was a Sunday camp; the Cooleys' wagons on one side, ours on the other; in the grove between them the table and chairs were set and the hammock hung in the shade. The camp stove stood a little way apart over cooling ashes. Farther away the horses were tied under the trees, and behind the wagons were screened places for our Saturday baths.

We must stay within sight or at least within hearing if our mothers called us, but as soon as morning tasks were done we were free to play in the woods. All day we climbed trees, picked berries, ate unripe walnuts and hazel-nuts, cracked between two stones. We startled rabbits that we must not chase far; we watched squirrels and birds, beetles and anthills. The hot air was full of good smells of rotting logs, dusty weeds, damp underneaths of mats of last year's oakleaves. Dandelion stems curled bitter on my tongue's tip and the green curls wilted over my ears.

Sharp flat stones were thick underfoot; we stubbed our toes

on them and all our big toes were wrapped in rags. Stone-bruises on our summer-calloused heels didn't stop our running. We found toadstools and mosses like teeny-tiniest forests, flat greenish-grey lichen on rocks, little perfect skins of locusts, empty, thin and brittle, clinging with tiny claws to the bark.

We picked up strange stones. When I showed my father a thin triangular one, wavy all over and sharp-pointed, he said it was an Indian arrowhead. We collected dozens of them and Paul found a stone axe-head.

One day I had to stay in camp with Mrs Cooley, I must mind her and not go out of her sight. My father had found a place, my mother was going with him to see it, and they wanted no worry about me while they were gone. There never had been such a long morning. I was embarrassed and so was Mrs Cooley. When at last I saw the team coming, my father and mother coming back, I felt like exploding; I could hardly be still and not speak until spoken to.

My father was glowing and my mother shining. She never had talked so fast. Just what they wanted, she told Mrs Cooley, so much, much more than they'd hoped for. A year-round spring of the best water you ever drank, a snug log house, in woods, on a hill, only a mile and a half from town so Rose could walk to school, and to cap all just think! four hundred young apple trees, heeled in, all ready to set out when the land was cleared. They'd bought it, as soon as dinner was over they were going to the bank to sign the papers. We were moving out that afternoon.

When he was excited my father always held himself quiet and steady, moving and speaking with deliberation. Some-times my quick mother flew out at him, but this day she was soft and warm. She left him eating at the camp table, told me to clear it and wash the dishes when he was through, and went into the screened place to get ready to meet the banker.

I perched on a stump and watched her brush out her hair

and braid it. She had beautiful hair, roan-brown, very fine and thick. Unbraided, it shimmered down to her heels; it was so long that when it was tightly braided she could sit on the braids. Usually it hung down her back in one wide braid but when she dressed up she must put up her hair and endure the headache.

Now she wound the braid around and around into a big mass on the back of her head, and fastened it with her tortoise-shell pins. She fluffed her bangs into a soft little mat in front, watching her comb in the small looking-glass fastened to a tree, and suddenly I realized that she was whistling; I remembered that I hadn't heard her whistling lately.

'Whistling girls and crowing hens always come to some bad ends,' she'd say gaily. She was whistling always. She whistled like a bird whistling a tune, clear and soft, clear and sweet, trilling, chirping, or dropping notes one by one as a meadow lark drops them from the sky. I was pleased to hear her whistling again.

Whistling, she buttoned up her new shoes with the button-hook. She took off her calico dress and folded it neatly. Standing in her bleached muslin petticoats and corset cover trimmed with crocheted lace, she took her best dress, her black cloth wedding dress, out of the box in which it had travelled from Dakota. Whistling, Oh Susanna, don't you cry for me, she put on the skirt and smoothed the placket. I was sorry that the skirt hid her new shoes. She coaxed her arms into the basque's tight sleeves and carefully buttoned all the glittery jet buttons up its front to her chin. With her gold pin she pinned the fold of ribbon, robin's-egg blue, to the front of the stand-up collar. Then, the very last thing, the climax: she pinned on her black sailor hat with the blue ribbon around the crown and the spray of wheat standing straight up at one side. The braids in back tilted the hat forward just a little; in front, the narrow brim rested on the mat of bangs.

She looked lovely; she was beautiful. You could see my father think so, when she came out and he looked at her.

She told him to hurry or they'd be late, but she spoke as if she were singing, not cross at all. He went into the screened place to change his shirt and comb his hair and moustache, and put on his new hat. To me my mother said that I could clear the table now, be sure to wash every dish while they were gone and, as usual, she told me to be careful not to break one. I never had broken a dish.

I remember all this so clearly because of what happened. I had taken away the dishes and wiped the table. My mother put down on it her clean handkerchief and her little red cloth pocketbook with the mother-of-pearl sides; she was wearing her kid gloves. Carefully she brought the writing desk and set it on the table. She laid back its slanted upper half and lifted out the narrow wooden tray that held the pen and inkwell.

The hundred dollar bill was gone.

There was a shock, like stepping in the dark on a top step that isn't there. But it could not be true. It was true; the place in the desk was empty. Everything changed. In the tight strangeness my father and mother were not like them; I did not feel like me.

They asked, Had I told anyone? Had I never said anything to anyone, ever, about that money? No. Had I seen a stranger near the wagon when they were not there? No. Or in camp? No.

My mother said it wasn't possible; not the Cooleys. My father agreed, no, not them. It *must* be there. My mother had seen it last in Kansas.

They took every sheet of writing paper out of the desk and shook it; they took each letter out of its envelope, unfolded it, looked into the empty envelope. They turned the desk upside down and shook it, the felt-covered inside lids flapping. My mother said they were losing their senses. Suddenly she thought, hoped, asked, Had I taken it myself, to play with?

NO! I felt scalded. She asked, Was I sure? I hadn't just opened the desk sometime, for fun? My throat swelled shut; I shook my head, no. 'Don't cry,' she said automatically. I wouldn't cry, I never cried, I was insulted, miserable, I was not a baby who'd play with money or open that desk for fun, I was going on eight years old. I was little, alone and scared. My father and mother sat there, still. In the long stillness I sank slowly into nothing but terror, pure terror without cause or object, a nightmare terror.

Finally my mother said, 'Well.' She meant, No use crying over spilled milk. What can't be cured must be endured. My father told her not to blame herself, it wasn't her fault. Carefully she peeled off her thin kid gloves. She turned them right-side-out finger by finger, smoothed them. She said that he'd better go explain to the banker.

Somehow the worst was over when he tried to put it off, saying something might turn up, and she flared out that he knew as well as she did, 'nothing turns up that we don't turn up ourselves.' Then she told me to run away and play, and I remembered the unwashed dishes. She had forgotten them.

For days, I don't remember how many days, everything was the same as ever and not at all the same. I said nothing about the disaster; I didn't want to. My mother told Mrs Cooley that they thought best to take time and make up their minds. My father looked for work in town. My mother knew nobody there. Mr Cooley sold one of his teams and one wagon; and Paul and George were going to move into the hotel and help run it. I knew we could sell the horses, but what then? Covered wagons were going by every day, going both ways as usual, some camping overnight nearby. Often I tried to think what would happen when we had nothing to eat; I couldn't.

Blackberries were fewer now and smaller. I was deep in the

briary patch, hunting them, when my mother called, and called again before I could get out without tearing my dress on the clutching thorns and run over the sharp stones to the camp. My father was hitching up, my mother was putting last things into the wagon. They had bought the farm. She had found the hundred dollar bill. In the writing desk. The jolting had slipped it into a crack in the desk and I was to stop asking questions and get into the wagon. Just as she was, my mother had found my father and gone to sign the papers, and just as I was, without even washing my feet, I was to obey her and get up onto that wagon seat, *now*, and no more words about it.

The town began with two small houses on a side road in the woods. Then there were two big houses in large yards with trees, and a cunning little low house right at the edge of the gravel sidewalk. On the other side of the road, opposite the little house, stairs went up the side of the hotel where Paul and George would live. In front of the hotel was the Square, with trees in it and lines of hitching posts around it, except on the far side where the railroad track was. We were driving along Main Street, and it was on one side of us and in front of us and behind us, too; it went around three sides of the Square. It was three solid rows of stores behind three high board sidewalks. This was The Gem City of the Ozarks.

We passed a big Reynolds General Store, with two large windows full of things, the door between them. Men were loafing, whittling, talking and spitting along the high board walk. There were small stores, The Bank of Mansfield, a Boston Racket Store with 'Opera House' painted on the windows upstairs, Hoover's Livery Stable and horses in a feed lot, then another big house inside a wire fence. Past a blacksmith shop the dusty road went downhill to cross a little bridge. The long hillside was orchard and pasture but houses began where the road went up again beyond the bridge. In all there must have been a dozen houses, in fenced yards with gates, behind paths through the weeds on both sides of the road.

All the houses had front porches; all were painted and trimmed with different colours and wooden lace. Behind them were vegetable gardens and clotheslines, barns and chicken houses; some had pigpens. Two had an upstairs; one of these had a bay window and a cupola. Behind the houses on our right was the railroad embankment; behind those on the left, two more houses and a high grassy hill against the sky.

At the top of the road's long climb stood the schoolhouse where I would go to school. It stood square, two storeys high, with windows all around, and its bell tower up above the double doors. All beyond it was woods; it was in the edge of the woods but not a single stump remained on the ground trodden bare and hard about it. There was a well beside it; behind it a woodshed and two privies: Boys and Girls.

I looked as long as I could, but the road turned away from the schoolhouse to follow the railroad track. The wheel tracks went beside the iron rails with the row of poles holding a telegraph wire on glass knobs above them. There were two houses in the woods; then the road turned into the woods and left the railroad behind us.

Now there was nothing but woods on either side, and the two wheel tracks went straight and slowly downward. Between them were stumps and big rocks. The wagon jolted and lurched over rocks in the dust and the horses' iron shoes clattered on them.

From the talk over my head I learned how lucky it was that the last cent had been just enough to pay for the salt pork and cornmeal. We could make out all right now, selling wood, and do well when the apple trees were in bearing. Paying off the mortgage would be easy then. Three hundred dollars at twelve per cent, pounded every three months. (Why would they be pounded? I wondered.) My mother could do arithmetic in her head. They ought to be able to carry it if they kept their health.

Either then or later I learned from such talk that some very foolish man had bought all those little apple trees from a smart salesman though he had no cleared land. When they came in their bundles, he had no clearing to set them out in; but he had signed papers, so he had to mortgage the land to pay for them. Then he just gave up. Between two days, he left the land and the cabin, the little apple trees root-buried in a trench, and the mortgage. So my father and mother got them from the banker.

The road went up again, it seemed to go almost vertically up a long, long hill, but my father turned the horses away from it, onto a fainter track in a valley. Beside us now a stream of water as clear as glass ran over flat ledges and through shallow pools. In a little while the wagon tracks turned to ford a pool. The horses stopped to drink and my mother said, 'Here we are!' She asked me what I thought of it, but I saw nothing to think about. The creek came from our own spring, she told me. Across the creek the woods went up a low hill in the yellow light of the sinking sun; the wheel tracks went on down the curve of the creek and trees hid them.

My father drove up the hill through the woods. The horses climbed clumsily, the flat rocks slipping under their feet. At the top of the hill we came into a tiny clearing at the edge of a deep ravine, and there stood a little log house.

Quick as a squirrel, I was down over the wheel and around the corner of logs' ends. A rough, thick door stood open; I was in the house, I was in a narrow little room, its floor of earth and dead leaves, but beyond a doorway was a large room that had a wooden floor. This room was bare and clean, it smelled like the woods, dead leaves were blown into its corners. There was a big fireplace and sure enough, no windows. There was a square hole in the wall of peeled logs; an empty hole, but it had a rough wooden door hanging open, like the house door.

Nothing more was to be seen there. But I hadn't noticed that in the narrow room the logs of the wall around the door were papered with newspapers. Large black letters in curleycues stopped me; I stood and read: 'Carter's Little Liver Pills', and a philosophical question which I kept trying and failing to answer for so long afterward that I have never forgotten it: What is life without a liver?

That problem was too much for me: for the moment, I postponed the struggle with it. Outside, some chunks of bark had fallen from the house wall, and between all the logs was yellow clay, dry and hard and cracked to bits. Not far away the path from the door went down, steeper than stairs, into the ravine. As usual, my mother called to me to be careful.

The ravine was shadowy, darker in its narrow bottom. It ended in one huge rock as big as a big house. Behind the rock was a hollow sound of running water, and water ran from beneath it into a little pool as round as a washtub and half as deep. Ferns hung over the darling pool, and from a bough above it dangled a hollowed-out gourd for dipping up the water.

I drank a delicious cold gourdful, looking up and up the mountainside above the spring. It was all dark woods, only the very tips of the highest trees in sudden yellow light. All down the dark ravine the water chuckled eerily. Something moved stealthily in the leaves under the bushes. I clambered up the path as fast as I could.

The horses were unhitched and picketed, the hens in their coop on the ground. My father and mother were taking out things over the wagon's opened endgate. We could eat supper outdoors and sleep one more night in the wagon. My mother meant to scrub that cabin floor from top to bottom before we moved into it. We could still see well enough in the shadowy daylight but inside the wagon it was too dark to find things. My father rummaged for the lantern.

He pressed the spring that lifted its thick glass globe, he touched the match-flame to the wick and carefully lowered the globe into its place, and suddenly the lantern was shining in darkness. He held it up, looking for a place to hang it, and there in the edge of its light stood a strange man.

The man's feet were bare, his pants were patched over patches and torn. He was tall, thin, bony, and his eyes glittered from a bush of hair and whiskers. He came a step nearer and quick as a snake my mother's hand slid into the pocket where her revolver was. She waited, ready. Slowly my father said, 'Hello there.'

The man said he wanted work, he was looking for a chance to work for something to eat. My father answered that we were just moving in, as he could see; we didn't have work to give anybody. Too bad, but maybe better luck in town, just over the next hill, not much more than a mile to the west.

'You got a good place here,' the man said. He was bony, but big. After a minute my father said it would be a good place someday, he guessed. Then we all stood silent as if we couldn't move.

The man began to talk quietly, slowly, almost dreamily. They had to get something to eat, he said. His wife and five children were down in the wagon by the creek. They had been travelling all summer looking for work. They could not go on any longer. This was the third day they'd had nothing to eat. He had to get work, so he came up the wagon tracks –

They couldn't go on without something to eat.

He stopped, there was nothing more to say. Nothing to do. Now I knew what happened when you had nothing to eat. What happens is, nothing.

Suddenly, my father was talking and moving quickly, not deliberate at all. He said he needed help making wood, provided the man would come help him tomorrow, he'd divide what little – He was reaching into the wagon. At sight of the slab of salted fat pork my mother cried out, 'Manly, *no! We've got Rose.*' He paid no attention. The butcher knife in his hand cut through the white meat. He opened a corner of the sack and poured cornmeal into the little tin pail. He was asking, did the man have a good axe? He said they'd start early, at sun-up, put in a good day's work and if the wood sold he'd treat the man right. Bring an axe if he had one. Be sure to bring back the pail. That's all right, don't mention it, see you tomorrow.

The man was gone into the darkness. He had not said a word. Afterward my mother always said that she expected never to see that vagabond again, nor her tin pail, either. At the time she said nothing. My father made the fire under the camp stove and she cooked supper. We had fried salt pork and corndodgers, and slept in the wagon.

The man woke us in the false dawn, bringing the tin pail and his axe. He was a better woodsman than my father. All that day while my mother and I cleaned the house and lugged things from the wagon to put on the dry, scrubbed floor, they worked in the woods. They worked as long as they could see. Then my mother held the lantern and they took the top and curtains off the wagon, and stacked up high in it all the stove wood that it would hold.

Early next morning my father set out to sell the wood in town. The man worked with a will while he was gone. He was gone all day. At night he had not come. The strange man went down the hill, my mother lighted the lamp, turned low to save kerosene. Still it was some time before we heard the wagon jolting. My mother lighted the lantern, then said I'd better take it to him.

I rushed out with it. The wagon box was empty and I almost shouted, 'You sold it!'

'Finally I did,' my father said in triumph.

'How much did you get for it?' I asked. He was beginning to unharness the horses. He bragged, 'Fifty cents.'

I set down the lantern and ran into the house to tell my mother, 'Fifty cents! He sold it all for fifty cents!' Her whole face trembled and seemed to melt into softness, she sighed a long sigh. 'Aren't you glad?' I exulted.

'Glad? Of course I'm glad!' she snapped at me and to herself, 'Oh, thanks be!'

I ran out again, I pranced out, to tell my father how glad she was. And he said, with a sound of crying in his voice, 'Oh, why did you tell her? I wanted to surprise her.'

You do such things, little things, horrible, cruel, without thinking, not meaning to. You have done it; nothing can undo it. This is a thing you can never forget.

How long that man worked with my father I don't remember. I cannot remember his name nor anything at all about his family camping down by the creek. Surely I knew those children; they must have been there for weeks. I remember that he and my father were roofing the little log barn, the day I chased the rabbit.

The leaves had fallen from all the trees but the oaks then, and the oaks wore their winter red that day. There was light snow or frost underfoot, so cold that it burned my bare feet, and my breath puffed white in the air. I chased that rabbit over the hills, up and down and back again until, exhausted, it hid in a hollow log; I stopped up the log's ends with rocks and fetched both men from their work on the roof to chop out the rabbit and kill it.

The day was Saturday; I was going to school then. For Sunday dinner we had rabbit stew, with gravy on mashed potatoes and on our cornbread. And on Monday I found in my lunch-pail at school one of that rabbit's legs; my mother had saved it and packed it with the cornbread in the little tin pail, to surprise me.

The man and his family must have gone on west or south, early that winter. He must have earned provisions for the trip. I remember walking to school through the snowy woods in my shoes and stockings, hearing the thuds of my father's axe sounding fainter as I went; and coming home with the sunset red behind me to hear the whirr-whirr of the crosscut saw growing sharper in the frosty air. The axe was too heavy for my mother; my father would not trust her with its sharpness, but she could safely handle one end of the crosscut saw.

Winter evenings were cosy in the cabin. The horses were warm in the little barn, the hens in the new wooden coop. Snow banked against the log walls and long icicles hung from the eaves. A good fire of hickory logs burned in the fireplace. In its heat, over a newspaper spread on the hearth, my father worked oil into the harness-straps between his oily-black hands. I sat on the floor, carefully building a house of corncobs, and my mother sat by the table, knitting needles flashing while she knitted warm woollen socks for my father and read to us from a book propped under the kerosene lamp. She read us Tennyson's poems and Scott's poems; those books were ours. And she read us Prescott's *Conquest of Mexico*, and *Conquest of Peru*, and *The Green Mountain Boys*, and *John Halifax, Gentleman*. She read us *The Leatherstocking Tales*, and another true book, the biggest of all: *Ancient, Medieval and Modern History*. I borrowed those from the shelf of lending-books in the Fourth Reader room at school. The teachers let me borrow them, though I wasn't in the Fourth Reader yet.

I remember the Sunday afternoon when my father and mother planned the new house. We had got the cow that spring: I must have been ten years old, going on eleven. On Sunday afternoons in warm weather, when company wasn't spending the day with us or we were not spending it in town with the Cooleys, my father and mother in their Sunday clothes went walking sedately over the land while I, in mine, minded the cabin. They had cleared twenty acres and set out all the little apple trees, and we had the cow, that Sunday afternoon when they decided where to build the house.

From my swing in the oak tree by the cabin, Fido and I saw them standing and talking under the huge old white-oak tree not far away. They talked a long while. Then my father went to lead the cow to water and change her picket-peg, and my mother called me to see the spot where our house would be.

It would be under the great old white-oak at the edge of the hill where we stood. Here the ground sloped more gently down into the ravine and rose steeply up the wooded mountain to the south. You could see the brook running from the widening mouth of the ravine and curving to the north and east around the base of the rounded hill. You could hear the water rippling over the limestone ledges. It was springtime; the hickory trees on the hill were in young green leaves, the oak leaves were pink, and all the flinty ground beneath them was covered with one blue-purple mat of dog's-tooth violets. Along the brook the sarvice trees were blooming misty white. The ancient white-oak was lively with dozens of young squirrels whisking into and out of their nests in the hollow branches.

My mother stood under it in her brown-sprigged white lawn dress, her long braid hanging down her back. Below the curled bangs her eyes were as purple-blue as the violets. It would be a white house, she said, all built from our farm. Everything we needed to build it was on the land: good oak beams and boards, stones for the foundation and the fireplace. The house would have large windows looking west across the brook, over the gentle little valley and up the wooded hills that hid the town, to the sunset colours in the sky. There would be a nice big porch to the north, cool on hot summer afternoons.

The kitchen would be big enough to hold a wood stove for winter and one of the new kerosene stoves that wouldn't heat up the place worse in summer. Every window would be screened with mosquito netting. There would be a well, with a pump, just outside the kitchen door; no more lugging water from the spring. And in the parlour there would be a bookcase, no, *two* bookcases, big bookcases full of books, and a hanging lamp to read them by, in winter evenings by the fireplace.

When the mortgage is paid, in only a few more years, she said, and when the orchard is in bearing, if prices are good then, we will fence the whole place with wire and build the barn bigger; we will have more stock by then. And after that, we can begin to build the house.

She woke from the dream with a start and a Goodness! it's chore-time! I'd better take the milk pail to my father, she said, and feed the hens before they went to roost; don't forget to fill their water-pans, and bring in the eggs; be careful not to break one. Oh, now that we had the cow, we'd have a treat for Sunday supper, French toast with that wild honey, to surprise my father. How wonderful it was to have a cow again.

While I scattered corn for the hens, fetched water from the spring to fill their pans, and hunted for eggs that the broody hens hid in the haymow, in the straw stack, and even in the wild grasses, I heard her whistling in the cabin, getting supper.